Karl Henning Carlson
N. Y. 12/11/11

"POSSON JONE'"
AND
PÈRE RAPHAËL

"POSSON JONE'"
AND
PÈRE RAPHAËL

WITH A
NEW WORD SETTING FORTH HOW AND WHY
THE TWO TALES ARE ONE

BY
GEORGE W. CABLE

ILLUSTRATED BY
STANLEY M. ARTHURS

NEW YORK
CHARLES SCRIBNER'S SONS
1909

ILLUSTRATIONS

v

INTRODUCTION

INTRODUCTION

A FEW months ago I stood once more in Royal Street, New Orleans, where all about me the very names of the thoroughfares have a quaint flavor of age and poetry. I mean half-way down between Canal Street and that small garden which, at the head of Or'.eans, between St. Peter and St. Ann, so pleasantly adorns the rear end, the good old Spanish end, of St. Louis cathedral.

The half-way corner where I paused, say a short quarter of a mile from Canal Street behind me and that garden before, was of particular interest to me because of my having taken, long ago, a story-teller's liberty with it, to the extent of pinching back the

INTRODUCTION

architectural history of one of its buildings
some seven years in order to accommodate
my friends Parson Jones and Jules St.-Ange;
a thing I hardly would have done for any
one else in the world, except, of course, the
present reader.

But there was a further reason for my
halt. I was at that special cross-roads to
try if the spot itself would not show me how
to make as plain to the reader, before he
should begin to read them, as it has always
been to the author, the fact that the printing
of these two stories together is a requirement
of their veritable unity, their essential one-
ness, a genuine love-match, made in heaven,
as lovers say, and bred of an affinity back
of all time!

With this purpose in mind, latent per-
haps, but "in being," I paused to gaze on

the startling change going on across the
way, where Dimitry Davezac a scant cen-
tury ago hovered for a glimpse of Abigail at
some front window of Jules's home in that
same Sabbath morning hour in which St.-
Ange and the West Floridian parson met,
at the capture of the latter's runaway hat.
On that side the buildings of an entire
square—Andrew Jackson's headquarters,
Gottschalk's birthplace, the shops of the
comb-mender and the pawnbroker, with all
the other structures, tall or squat, around
which, that morning, went Jules and the
Parson into the Rue Chartres on their absurd
circuit to Miguel's gambling-den—were gone,
wiped off the earth forever, and in their place
was rising one vast, beautiful marble palace
of justice (human justice), wherein all the
tribunals of the stupendously expanded city

will ere long be housed together. I could not resent the metamorphosis, yet I was glad that I had found here, before the renovation came, not one story alone, but two, and they spiritually twins, occupying the same place at the same time, life-mated long before the birth of either, and this equally by the spot's ancient romantic warrant and by the modernest court sanction; for there stood the courts, silent, and by their own immemorial ruling silence is assent.

I say by the spot's warrant of antiquity, romance, and picturesque decay, for this I had already realized at nearly every step of my approach, and especially at one point only a few yards behind me. I had found the persistently warm, moist air still laying its pathetic touch of premature age and decline on every wall and roof that betrayed

the slightest neglect, and still that touch was
half redeemed by the complacent oblivious-
ness to it of tenant, landlord, and the general
eye; while historic interest, eccentricity of
architectural lines, and bravery of color on
masonry and carpentry and in human dress
and adornment maintained as ever their
quaint pre-eminence. In "Père Raphaël"
there is mention of wide archways. At the
point I name I had noted one of these opening inward from the sidewalk by high
double-leaved doors of dingy green iron
openwork. The passage within, some eight
feet broad, was colored a strong terra-cotta
hue the first four feet up from its stone flagging, and then white maybe eight feet more
to the bright green ceiling. It ended in a
second arch some forty feet away, whose
openwork gates, still handsomer than the

[7]

near ones, were of wrought iron and, standing wide, laid the dark lace of their pattern
against the two white and terra-cotta walls.
Beyond lay a small, square, flagged court
deeply shut in all round by lofty buildings.
At its farther bound a heavy green batten
door, broad, high, arched, and grimly ironed,
but open, showed an interior whose rich
brown half-light revealed rising tiers of wine
casks of the same color in livelier tints. In
the court, beside the door, a stack of yellow
wine cases stood against a wall of smoky
white stucco with large peeled-away blotches
of age-softened red brickwork picked out
with the gray of its crumbling mortar. Above
these cases an iron-barred window, twice as
wide as it was high, a sort of huge transom,
occupied much of the wall, yet showed only
darkness behind it. I might admit that for

striking effect the moment was fortunate, were it not that in that region I have never known when it was not fortunate. At any rate, the court's green-brown flagging was shining wet, and repeated all those good lines and daring colors in its mirror. A man in dark trousers and a navy-blue shirt came out of the wine-room, bearing by its hand-holes another of those yellow cases of bottled wine or ale to the stack; and on the same instant, as if Dame Fortune had turned stage manager, verily, at a leisurely untimorous trot, a coal-black cat picked her steps across the wet court from some ferns and tropical shrubberies against one side wall to others on the opposite boundary.

Do you notice how exclusively masculine was the whole scene? Its one poor hint of do-mesticity was the cat, and she, like enough, was but a warehouse cat after all. As lonesomely masculine it all was as the tale of "Posson Jone'." And then see what followed. The perfection of the picture, except for this one subtle drawback, argued the improbability that there could be anything to match it near by, yet moved me, as I went on, to go with seeking eyes, and I had not left the sight five steps behind when I found its consort! Oh, mark you! this is no builded fiction, but the clean sand of fact as I noted it down right there lest later I *might* let imagination impose on memory. This second archway and court had batten gates at their sidewalk front, with a batten wicket in one of them. The arcade was colored brown and terra-cotta. In the court was a riot of palm, rubber, and banana foliage, with banks and hanging-baskets of ferns, and under the arch

that curved between these and the dark archway, against the luminous greenery, and with
a fine old lamp and crane of wrought iron
overhanging their heads, sat three women of
the household, in rocking-chairs, sewing. I
could not turn my back so promptly and
make believe to be taking my pencil notes
from across the way, but a young man came
with the firm step and polite emphasis of a
Davezac and shut the wicket. The tale of
"Père Raphaël" was justified.

A story-teller does not so much make a
story as find it. He finds the stone, he cuts
the gem. Stories, like wild flowers, are the
product of the soil that favors them, and I
have my own experience in this very case
to show that a soil has only to be rich
enough in order for one story to become two
and yet the two to remain one. Also to

show, twice proved, that the story-teller is
most likely to find the sort of story he is
looking for. "Posson Jone'" is a story of
love, yet not, in its initial singleness, a love
story. I found it because I was distinctively
seeking one that should portray an ardent
and controlling mutual affection springing
into life wholly apart from the passion of
sex; flowering out of the pure admiration of
two masculine characters for their utter
opposites, and overcoming all the separative
distance that could be made by antipodal
conditions of nationa ity, religious training,
political sentiment, native temperament,
years, and social quality and tradition.

As fulfilling these conditions "Posson
Jone'" so satisfied my easily pleased fancy
and found its way so steadily, though slowly,
into the favor of readers, that for years it did

INTRODUCTION

not occur to me that another story of the
same time, place, and circumstance might be
lying beneath it, like one painting beneath
another in the same frame and on the same
canvas, or like one fireplace around another
in some big chimney of an old mansion.
I doubt if I should ever have thought of it
had I not been kept many years in the clos-
est companionship of Jules and the Parson
by the flattering willingness of public audi-
ences to hear their episode recounted; but
through this ever-growing intimacy the be-
lief, so to call it, came and its reasonableness
argued for it. It seemed hardly rational to
go on assuming that two souls so fitly
made for loving and so prompt and glad to
love that their worship of moral strength and
beauty could carry their affections over such
a gulf of dissimilarity should not have, operat-

[13]

ing potentially in their daily lives, that most universal of all love's forms, the grand passion. Parson Jones was probably already a husband or a widower; but Jules was young, handsome, single, a Latin, and a Creole. At that phase of my thought one circumstance of the tale after another rose up in confirming evidence, and the moment the author accused his blithe hero of having another story, as you might say, concealed on his person the blithe Creole brought it forth as frankly as, a hundred years ago, he had produced his card-table spoils to Parson Jones on the banks of Bayou St. John.

With only the pleasantest feelings I recognize that many a kind friend of Jones and Jules will resent what at first blush they may suspect to be an arbitrary yoking of that pair with Florestine, Dimitry, and Abigail, and

[14]

will declare without granting so much as a
preliminary hearing that the tale of these
latter is not the tale of the former. But,
queerly enough, that is almost precisely
what was originally said, by one of the leading editors of our land, concerning the *first*
story, when declining it for his magazine:
that *it* was not the right story, inasmuch
as it was not a love story. In fact, Posson
Jone' had a hard time getting into print,
went bowing and scraping from editorial
door to door, and on being printed, was received with as quiet a neglect as any rustic
could be. A year or so later, on the first
issuance of "Old Creole Days," with Jones
and Jules in it, one noted critic and warm
friend was openly vexed that so poor a tale
as theirs should have been assigned—by
oversight—a place which he believed to be

of strategic value for the fortunes of the book; to wit, the end of the procession.

However, let us sum up in the one word, that this alliance is no *mariage de convenance*, whatever may be the two tales' disparity of years; though, if it were, our Gallic Jules would be the most likely of us all to take it as a matter of course and draw from it the fullest measure of delight. Here are the two stories joined in wedlock, and here their parent unfeignedly well pleased with the unavoidably delayed match, and harboring, after all, only the one fear that, in his eagerness to please everybody, he may be absurdly overestimating his reader's interest in the case. The one true test of the match's goodness is for the reader to read on with an open and charitable mind. If, at the volume's end, approval is no more apathetic than it was

INTRODUCTION

to each of the contracting parties separately
on their first appearance, the author will
venture to hope for them a long and happy
married life.

G. W. CABLE.

Northampton, Mass., July, 1909.

"POSSON JONE'"

In his arms he bore ... the tiger

"POSSON JONE'"

TO Jules St.-Ange—elegant little heathen—there yet remained at manhood a remembrance of having been sent to school, and of having been taught by a stony-headed Capuchin that the world is round—for example, like a cheese. This round world is a cheese to be eaten through, and Jules had nibbled quite into his cheese-world already at twenty-two.

He realized this as he idled about one Sunday morning where the intersection of Royal and Conti Streets some seventy years ago formed a central corner of New Orleans. Yes, yes, the trouble was he had been wasteful and honest. He discussed the matter with that faithful friend and confidant, Bap-

[21]

tiste, his yellow body-servant. They concluded that, papa's patience and *tante's* pin-
money having been gnawed away quite to
the rind, there were left open only these few
easily enumerated resorts: to go to work—
they shuddered; to join Major Innerarity's
filibustering expedition; or else—why not?
—to try some games of confidence. At
twenty-two one must begin to be something.
Nothing else tempted; could that avail?
One could but try. It is noble to try; and,
besides, they were hungry. If one could
"make the friendship" of some person from
the country, for instance, with money, not
expert at cards or dice, but, as one would
say, willing to learn, one might find cause to
say some "Hail Marys."

The sun broke through a clearing sky,
and Baptiste pronounced it good for luck.

[22]

There had been a hurricane in the night. The weed-grown tile-roofs were still dripping, and from lofty brick and low adobe walls a rising steam responded to the summer sunlight. Up-street, and across the Rue du Canal, one could get glimpses of the gardens in Faubourg Ste.-Marie standing in silent wretchedness, so many tearful Lucretias, tattered victims of the storm. Short remnants of the wind now and then came down the narrow street in erratic puffs heavily laden with odors of broken boughs and torn flowers, skimmed the little pools of rain-water in the deep ruts of the unpaved street, and suddenly went away to nothing, like a juggler's butterflies or a young man's money.

It was very picturesque, the Rue Royale. The rich and poor met together. The locksmith's swinging key creaked next door to the bank; across the way, crouching mendicant-like in the shadow of a great importing house, was the mud laboratory of the mender of broken combs. Light balconies overhung the rows of showy shops and stores open for trade this Sunday morning, and pretty Latin faces of the higher class glanced over their savagely pronged railings upon the passers below. At some windows hung lace curtains, flannel duds at some, and at others only the scraping and sighing one-hinged shutter groaning toward Paris after its neglectful master.

M. St.-Ange stood looking up and down the street for nearly an hour. But few ladies, only the inveterate mass-goers, were out. About the entrances of the frequent *cafés* the masculine gentility stood leaning

on canes, with which now one and now another beckoned to Jules, some even adding
pantomimic hints of the social cup.

M. St.-Ange remarked to his servant without turning his head that somehow he felt
sure he should soon return those *bons* that
the mulatto had lent him.

"What will you do with them?"

"Me!" said Baptiste, quickly; "I will go
and see the bull-fight in the Place Congo."

"There is to be a bull-fight? But where
is M. Cayetano?"

"Ah, got all his affairs wet in the tornado.
Instead of his circus, they are to have a bull-
fight— not an ordinary bull-fight with sick
horses, but a buffalo-and-tiger fight. I
would not miss it——"

Two or three persons ran to the opposite corner and began striking at some-

[25]

thing with their canes. Others followed. Can M. St.-Ange and servant, who hasten forward—can the Creoles, Cubans, Spaniards, St. Domingo refugees, and other loungers—can they hope it is a fight? They hurry forward. Is a man in a fit? The crowd pours in from the side-streets. Have they killed a so-long snake? Bareheaded shopmen leave their wives, who stand upon chairs. The crowd huddles and packs. Those on the outside make little leaps into the air, trying to be tall.

"What is the matter?"

"Have they caught a real live rat?"

"Who is hurt?" asks some one in English.

"*Personne*," replies a shopkeeper; "a man's hat blow' in the gutter; but he has it now. Jules pick it. See, that is the man, head and shoulders on top the res'."

"He in the homespun?" asks a second shopkeeper. "Humph! an *Américain*—a West-Floridian; bah!"

"But wait; 'st! he is speaking; listen!"

"To who' is he speak——?"

"Sh-sh-sh! to Jules."

"Jules who?"

"Silence, you! To Jules St.-Ange, what h-owe me a bill since long time. Sh-sh-sh!"

Then the voice was heard.

Its owner was a man of giant stature, with a slight stoop in his shoulders, as if he were making a constant, good-natured attempt to accommodate himself to ordinary doors and ceilings. His bones were those of an ox. His face was marked more by weather than age, and his narrow brow was bald and smooth. He had instantaneously formed an opinion of Jules St.-Ange, and the multitude of words, most of them lingual curiosities, with which he was rasping the wide-open ears of his listeners, signified, in short, that, as sure as his name was Parson Jones, the little Creole was a "plumb gentleman."

M. St.-Ange bowed and smiled, and was about to call attention, by both gesture and speech, to a singular object on top of the still uncovered head, when the nervous motion of the *Américain* anticipated him, as, throwing up an immense hand, he drew down a large roll of bank-notes. The crowd laughed, the West-Floridian joining, and began to disperse.

"Why, that money belongs to Smyrny Church," said the giant.

"You are very dengerous to make your money expose like that, Misty Posson Jone'," said St.-Ange, counting it with his eyes.

The countryman gave a start and smile of surprise.

"How d'd you know my name was Jones?" he asked; but, without pausing for the Creole's answer, furnished in his reckless way some further specimens of West-Floridian English; and the conciseness with which he presented full intelligence of his home, family, calling, lodging-house, and present and future plans, might have passed for consummate art, had it not been the most run-wild nature. "And I've done been to Mobile, you know, on bus*iness* for Bethesdy Church. It's the on'yest time I ever been from home; now you wouldn't of believed that, would you? But I admire to have saw you, that's so. You've got to come and eat with me. Me and my boy ain't been fed yit. What might one call yo' name? Jools? Come on,

Jools. Come on, Colossus. That's my niggah—his name's Colossus of Rhodes. Is
that yo' yallah boy, Jools? Fetch him along,
Colossus. It seems like a special prov*idence*.
—Jools, do you believe in a special provi-
dence? "

Jules remembered the roll of bank-notes
and said he did.

The new-made friends moved briskly off,
followed by Baptiste and a short, square,
old negro, very black and grotesque, who
had introduced himself to the mulatto, with
many glittering and cavernous smiles, as
"d'body-sarvant of d'Rev'n' Mr. Jones."

Both pairs enlivened their walk with conversation. Parson Jones descanted upon
the doctrine he had mentioned, as illustrated
in the perplexities of cotton-growing, and
concluded that there would always be "a

special provi*dence* again' cotton untell folks quits a-pressin' of it and haulin' of it on Sundays!"

"*Je dis*," said St.-Ange, in response, "I thing you is juz right. I believe, me, strong-strong in the improvidence, yes. You know my papa he h-own a sugah-plantation, you know. 'Jules, my son,' he say one time to me, 'I goin' to make one baril sugah to fedge the moze high price in New Orleans.' Well, he take his bez baril sugah—I nevah see a so careful man like my papa always to make a so beautiful sugah *et sirop*. 'Jules, go at Father Pierre an' ged this lill pitcher fill with holy-water, an' tell him sen' his tin bucket, and I will make it fill with *quitte*.' I ged the holy-water; my papa sprinkle it over the baril, an' make one cross on the 'ead of the baril."

"Why, Jools," said Parson Jones, "that didn't do no good."

"Din do no good! Id broughd the so great value! You can strike me dead if thad baril sugah din fedge the more high cost than any other in the city. *Parceque*, the man what buy that baril sugah he make a mistake of one hundred pound '"—falling back—"*Mais* certainlee!"

"And you think that was growin' out of the holy-water?" asked the parson.

"*Mais*, what could make it else? Id could not be the *quitte*, because my papa keep the bucket, an' forget to sen' the *quitte* to Father Pierre."

Parson Jones was disappointed.

"Well, now, Jools, you know, I don't think that was right. I reckon you must be a plumb Catholic."

M. St.-Ange shrugged. He would not deny his faith.

"I am a *Catholique, mais*"—brightening as he hoped to recommend himself anew— "not a good one."

"Well, you know," said Jones—"where's Colossus? Oh! all right. Colossus strayed off a minute in Mobile, and I plumb lost him for two days. Here's the place; come in. Colossus and this boy can go to the kitchen. —Now, Colossus, what *air* you a-beckonin' at me faw?"

He let his servant draw him aside and address him in a whisper.

"Oh, go 'way!" said the parson with a jerk. "Who's goin' to throw me? What? Speak louder. Why, Colossus, you shayn't talk so, saw. 'Pon my soul, yo're the mightiest fool I ever taken up with. Jest you go

[33]

down that alley-way with this yallah boy, and
don't show yo' face untell yo' called!"

The negro begged; the master wrathily
insisted.

"Colossus, will you do ez I tell you, or
shell I hev' to strike you, saw?"

"O Mahs Jimmy, I—I's gwine; but"—
he ventured nearer—"don't on no account
drink nothin', Mahs Jimmy."

Such was the negro's earnestness that he
put one foot in the gutter, and fell heavily
against his master. The parson threw him
off angrily.

"Thar, now! Why, Colossus, you most
of been dosted with sumthin'; yo' plumb
crazy. Humph, come on, Jools, let's eat:
Humph! to tell me that when I never taken
a drop, exceptin' for chills, in my life—
which he knows so as well as me!"

The two masters began to ascend a stair.

"*Mais*, he is a sassy; I would sell him, me," said the young Creole.

"No, I wouldn't do that," replied the parson; "though there is people in Bethesdy who says he is a roscal. He's a powerful smart fool. Why, that boy's got money, Jools; more money than religion, I reckon. I'm shore he fallen into mighty bad company"—they passed beyond earshot.

Baptiste and Colossus, instead of going to the tavern kitchen, went on to the next door and entered the dark rear corner of a low grocery, where, the law notwithstanding, liquor was covertly sold to slaves. There, in the quiet company of Baptiste and the grocer, the colloquial powers of Colossus, which were simply prodigious, began very soon to show themselves.

"For whilst," said he, "Mahs Jimmy has eddication, you know—whilst he has eddication, I has 'scretion. He has eddication and I has 'scretion, an' so we gits along."

He drew a black bottle down the counter, and, laying half his length upon the damp board, continued:

"As a p'inciple I discredits de imbimin' of awjus liquors. De imbimin' of awjus liquors, de wiolution of de Sabbaf, de playin' of de fiddle, and de usin' of by-words, dey is de fo' sins of de conscience; an' if any man sin de fo' sins of de conscience, de debble done sharp his fork fo' dat man.—Ain't dat so, boss?"

The grocer was sure it was so.

"Neberdeless, mind you"—here the orator brimmed his glass from the bottle and swallowed the contents with a dry eye—"mind

[36]

you, a roytious man, sech as ministers of de gospel and deir body-sarvants, can take a *leetle* for de weak stomach."

But the fascinations of Colossus's eloquence must not mislead us; this is the story of a true Christian; to wit, Parson Jones.

The parson and his new friend ate. But the coffee M. St.-Ange declared he could not touch; it was too wretchedly bad. At the French Market, near by, there was some noble coffee. This, however, would have to be bought, and Parson Jones had scruples.

"You see, Jools, every man has his conscience to guide him, which it does so in——"

"Oh, yes!" cried St.-Ange, "conscien'; thad is the bez, Posson Jone'. Certainlee! I am a *Catholique*, you is a *schismatique;* you thing it is wrong to dring some coffee—

well, then, it *is* wrong; you thing it is wrong
to make the sugah to ged the so large price
—well, then, it *is* wrong; I thing it is right
—well, then it *is* right; it is all 'abit; *c'est
tout*. What a man thing is right, *is right;* 'tis
all 'abit. A man muz nod go again' his conscien'. My faith! do you thing I would go
again' my conscien'? *Mais allons*, led us
go and ged some coffee."

"Jools."

"W'at?"

"Jools, it ain't the drinkin' of coffee, but
the buyin' of it on a Sabbath. You must
really excuse me, Jools, it's again' conscience, you know."

"Ah!" said St.-Ange, "*c'est* very true.
For you it would be a sin, *mais* for me it is
only 'abit. Rilligion is a very strange; I
know a man one time, he thing it was wrong

to go to cock-fight Sunday evening. I thing
it is all 'abit. *Mais*, come, Posson Jone';
I have got one friend, Miguel; led us go at
his house and ged some coffee. Come;
Miguel have no familie; only him and Joe—
always like to see friend; *allons*, led us come
yonder."

"Why, Jools, my dear friend, you know,"
said the shamefaced parson, "I never visit
on Sundays."

"Never w'at?" asked the astounded
Creole.

"No," said Jones, smiling awkwardly.

"Never visite?"

"Exceptin' sometimes amongst church-
members," said Parson Jones.

"*Mais*," said the seductive St.-Ange,
"Miguel and Joe is church-member'—certainlee! They love to talk about rilligion.

Come at Miguel and talk about some rilligion. I am nearly expire for my coffee."

Parson Jones took his hat from beneath
his chair and rose up.

"Jools," said the weak giant, "I ought to
be in church right now."

"*Mais*, the church is right yond' at
Miguel, yes. Ah!" continued St.-Ange, as
they descended the stairs, "I thing every
man muz have the rilligion he like the bez—
me, I like the *Catholique* rilligion the bez—
for me it *is* the bez. Every man will sure go
to heaven if he like his rilligion the bez."

"Jools," said the West-Floridian, laying
his great hand tenderly upon the Creole's
shoulder, as they stepped out upon the *ban-
quette*, "do you think you have any shore
hopes of heaven?"

"Yaas!" replied St.-Ange; "I am sure-

sure. I thing everybody will go to heaven. I thing you will go, *et* I thing Miguel will go, *et* Joe—everybody, I thing—*mais*, h-of course, not if they not have been christen'. Even I thing some niggers will go.'

"Jools," said the parson, stopping in his walk—"Jools, I *don't* want to lose my nig-gah."

"You will not loose him. With Baptiste he *cannot* ged loose."

But Colossus's master was not reassured.

"Now," said he, still tarrying, "this is jest the way; had I of gone to church——"

"Posson Jone'," said Jules.

"What?"

"I tell you. We goin' to church!"

"Will you?" asked Jones, joyously.

"*Allons*, come along," said Jules, taking his elbow.

They walked down the Rue Chartres, passed several corners, and by and by turned into a cross street. The parson stopped an instant as they were turning, and looked back up the street.

"W'at you lookin'?" asked his companion.

"I thought I saw Colossus," answered the parson, with an anxious face; "I reckon 'twa'n't him, though." And they went on.

The street they now entered was a very quiet one. The eye of any chance passer would have been at once drawn to a broad, heavy, white brick edifice on the lower side of the way, with a flag-pole standing out like a bowsprit from one of its great windows, and a pair of lamps hanging before a large closed entrance. It was a theatre, sub-let to gamblers. At this morning hour all was still,

[42]

and the only sign of life was a knot of little barefoot girls gathered within its narrow shade and each carrying an infant relative. Into this place the parson and M. St.-Ange entered, the little nurses jumping up from the sills to let them pass in.

A half-hour may have passed. At the end of that time the whole juvenile company were laying alternate eyes and ears to the chinks, to gather what they could of an interesting quarrel going on within.

"I did not, saw! I given you no cause of offence, saw! It's not so, saw! Mister Jools simply mistaken the house, thinkin' it was a Sabbath-school! No such thing, saw; I *ain't* bound to bet! Yes, I kin git out! Yes, without bettin'! I hev a right to my opinion; I reckon I'm *a white man*, saw! No, saw! I on'y said I didn't think you

could get the game on them cards. 'Sno
such thing, saw! I do *not* know how to play!
I wouldn't hev a roscal's money ef I should
win it! Shoot, ef you dare! You can kill me,
but you can't scare me! No, I shayn't bet!
I'll die first! Yes, saw; Mr. Jools can bet
for me if he admires to; I ain't his mostah."

Here the speaker seemed to direct his
words to St.-Ange.

"Saw, I don't understand you, saw.
I never said I'd loan you money to bet on me.
I didn't suspicion this from you, saw. No,
I won't take any mo' lemonade; it's the
most notorious stuff I ever drank, saw!"

M. St.-Ange's replies were in *falsetto* and
not without effect; for presently the parson's
indignation and anger began to melt. "Don't
ask me, Jools, I can't help you. It's no use;
it's a matter of conscience with me, Jools."

[44]

"Shoot, ef you dare! You can kill me, but you can't scare me!"

"*Mais oui!* 'tis a matt' of conscien' wid me, the same."

"But, Jools, the money's none o' mine, nohow; it belongs to Smyrny, you know."

"If I could make juz *one* bet," said the persuasive St.-Ange, "I would leave this place, fas'-fas', yes. If I had thing—*mais* I did not soupspicion this from you, Posson Jone'——"

"Don't, Jools, don't!"

"No! Posson Jone'."

"You're bound to win?" said the parson, wavering.

"*Mais certainement!* But it is not to win that I want; 'tis my conscien'—my honor!"

"Well, Jools, I hope I'm not a-doin' no wrong. I'll loan you some of this money if you say you'll come right out 'thout takin' your winnin's."

All was still. The peeping children could see the parson as he lifted his hand to his breast pocket. There it paused a moment in bewilderment, then plunged to the bottom. It came back empty, and fell lifelessly at his side. His head dropped upon his breast, his eyes were for a moment closed, his broad palms were lifted and pressed against his forehead, a tremor seized him, and he fell all in a lump to the floor. The children ran off with their infant loads, leaving Jules St.-Ange swearing by all his deceased relatives, first to Miguel and Joe, and then to the lifted parson, that he did not know what had become of the money "except if" the black man had got it.

In the rear of ancient New Orleans, beyond the sites of the old rampart, (a trio of

Spanish forts,) where the town has since sprung up and grown old, green with all the luxuriance of the wild Creole summer, lay the Congo Plains. Here stretched the canvas of the historic Cayetano, who Sunday after Sunday sowed the sawdust for his circus-ring.

But to-day the great showman had fallen short of his printed promise. The hurricane had come by night, and with one fell swash had made an irretrievable sop of everything. The circus trailed away its bedraggled magnificence, and the ring was cleared for the bull.

Then the sun seemed to come out and work for the people. "See," said the Spaniards, looking up at the glorious sky with its great white fleets drawn off upon the horizon—"see—heaven smiles upon the bull-fight!"

In the high upper seats of the rude amphitheatre sat the gayly decked wives and
daughters of the Gascons, from the *métairies*
along the Ridge, and the chattering Spanish
women of the Market, their shining hair
unbonneted to the sun. Next below were
their husbands and lovers in Sunday blouses,
milkmen, butchers, bakers, black-bearded
fishermen, Sicilian fruiterers, swarthy Portu-
guese sailors in little woollen caps, and
strangers of the graver sort; mariners of
England, Germany, and Holland. The low-
est seats were full of trappers, smugglers,
Canadian *voyageurs*, drinking and singing;
Américains, too—more's the shame—from
the upper rivers—who will not keep their
seats, who ply the bottle, and who will get
home by and by and tell how wicked Sodom
is; broad-brimmed, silver-braided Mexicans,

also, with their copper cheeks and bat's eyes,
and their tinkling spurred heels. Yonder, in
that quieter section, are the quadroon women
in their black lace shawls—and there is Baptiste; and below them are the turbaned
black women, and there is—but he vanishes
—Colossus.

The afternoon is advancing, yet the sport,
though loudly demanded, does not begin.
The *Américains* grow derisive and find pas-
time in gibes and raillery. They mock the
various Latins with their national inflections,
and answer their scowls with laughter.
Some of the more aggressive shout pretty
French greetings to the women of Gascony,
and one bargeman, amid peals of applause,
stands on a seat and hurls a kiss to the
quadroons. The mariners of England,
Germany, and Holland, as spectators, like

the fun, while the Spaniards look back and
cast defiant imprecations upon their perse-
cutors. Some Gascons, with timely caution,
pick their women out and depart, running a
terrible fire of gallantries.

In hope of truce, a new call is raised for
the bull: "The bull, the bull!—hush!"

In a tier near the ground a man is standing and calling—standing head and shoulders above the rest—calling in the *Améri-
caine* tongue. Another man, big and red,
named **Joe,** and a handsome little Creole in
elegant dress and full of laughter, wish to
stop him, but the flat-boatmen, ha-ha-ing
and cheering, will not suffer it. Ah, through
some shameful knavery of the men into
whose hands he has fallen, he is drunk!
Even the women can see that; and now he
throws his arms wildly and raises his voice

until the whole great circle hears it. He is preaching!

Ah! kind Lord, for a special providence now! The men of his own nation—men from the land of the open English Bible and temperance cup and song are cheering him on to mad disgrace. And now another call for the appointed sport is drowned by the flat-boatmen singing the ancient tune of Mear. You can hear the words—

" Old Grimes is dead, that good old soul "

—From ribald lips and throats turned brazen with laughter, from singers who toss their hats aloft and roll in their seats the chorus swells to the accompaniment of a thousand brogans—

" He used to wear an old gray coat
All buttoned down before. "

A ribboned man in the arena is trying to be heard, and the Latins raise one mighty cry for silence. The big red man gets a hand over the parson's mouth, and the ribboned man seizes his moment.

"They have been endeavoring for hours," he says, "to draw the terrible animals from their dens, but such is their strength and fierceness, that——"

His voice is drowned. Enough has been heard to warrant the inference that the beasts cannot be whipped out of the storm-drenched cages to which menagerie life and long starvation have attached them, and from the roar of indignation the man of ribbons flies. The noise increases. Men are standing up by hundreds, and women are imploring to be let out of the turmoil. All at once, like the bursting of a dam, the whole mass pours down into the ring. They sweep across the arena and over the showman's barriers. Miguel gets a frightful trampling. Who cares for gates or doors? They tear the beasts' houses bar from bar, and, laying hold of the gaunt buffalo, drag him forth by feet, ears, and tail; and in the midst of the *mêlée*, still head and shoulders above all, wilder, with the cup of the wicked, than any beast, is the man of God from the Florida parishes!

In his arms he bore—and all the people shouted at once when they saw it—the tiger. He had lifted it high up with its back to his breast, his arms clasped under its shoulders; the wretched brute had curled up caterpillar-wise, with its long tail against its belly, and through its filed teeth grinned a fixed and impotent wrath. And Parson Jones was shouting:

[53]

"The tiger and the buffler *shell* lay down together! You dah to say they shayn't and I'll comb you with this varmint from head to foot! The tiger and the buffler *shell* lay down together. They *shell*. Now, you, Joe! Behold! I am here to see it done. The lion and the buffler *shell* lay down together!"

Mouthing these words again and again, the parson forced his way through the surge in the wake of the buffalo. This creature the Latins had secured by a lariat over his head, and were dragging across the old rampart and into a street of the city.

The northern races were trying to prevent, and there was pommelling and knocking down, cursing and knife drawing, until Jules St.-Ange was quite carried away with the fun, laughed, clapped his hands, and swore with delight, and ever kept close to the gallant parson.

Joe, contrariwise, counted all this child's play an interruption. He had come to find Colossus and the money. In an unlucky moment he made bold to lay hold of the parson, but a piece of the broken barriers in the hands of a flat-boatman felled him to the sod, the terrible crowd swept over him, the lariat was cut, and the giant parson hurled the tiger upon the buffalo's back. In another instant both brutes were dead at the hands of the mob; Jones was lifted from his feet, and prating of Scripture and the millennium, of Paul at Ephesus and Daniel in the "buffler's" den, was borne aloft upon the shoulders of the huzzaing *Américains*. Half an hour later he was sleeping heavily on the floor of a cell in the *calaboza*.

[55]

When Parson Jones awoke, a bell was somewhere tolling for midnight. Somebody was at the door of his cell with a key. The lock grated, the door swung, the turnkey looked in and stepped back, and a ray of moonlight fell upon M. Jules St.-Ange. The prisoner sat upon the empty shackles and ring-bolt in the centre of the floor.

"Misty Posson Jone'," said the visitor, softly.

"O Jools!"

"*Mais*, w'at de matter, Posson Jone'?"

"My sins, Jools, my sins!"

"Ah! Posson Jone', is that something to cry, because a man get sometime a litt' bit intoxicate? *Mais*, if a man keep *all the time* intoxicate, I think that is again' the conscien'."

"Jools, Jools, your eyes is darkened—oh! Jools, where's my pore old niggah?"

A ray of moonlight fell upon M. Jules St.-Ange

"Posson Jone', never mine; he is wid Baptiste."

"Where?"

"I don' know w'ere—*mais* he is wid Baptiste. Baptiste is a beautiful to take care of somebody."

"Is he as good as you, Jools?" asked Parson Jones, sincerely.

Jules was slightly staggered.

"You know, Posson Jone', you know, a nigger cannot be good as a w'ite man— *mais* Baptiste is a good nigger."

The parson moaned and dropped his chin into his hands.

"I was to of left for home to-morrow, sun up, on the *Isabella* schooner. Pore Smyrny!" He sighed deeply.

"Posson Jone'," said Jules, leaning against the wall and smiling, "I swear you is the moz

funny man what I never see. If I was you I
would say, me, 'Ah! 'ow I am lucky! the
money I los', it was not mine, anyhow!' My
faith! shall a man make hisse'f to be the
more sorry because the money he los' is not
his? Me, I would say, 'it is a specious
providence.'

"Ah! Misty Posson Jone'," he continued, "you make a so droll sermon ad the
bull-ring. Ha! ha! I swear I thing you can
make money to preach thad sermon many
time ad the theatre St. Philippe. Hah! you
is the moz brave dat I never see, *mais* ad the
same time the moz rilligious man. Where
I'm goin' to fin' one priest to make like dat?
Mais, why you can't cheer up an' be 'appy?
Me, if I should be miserabl' like dat I would
kill meself."

The countryman only shook his head.

"*Bien*, Posson Jone', I have the so good news for you."

The prisoner looked up with eager inquiry.

"Laz' evening when they lock' you, I come right off at M. De Blanc's house to get you let out of the calaboose; M. De Blanc he is the judge. So soon I was entering— 'Ah! Jules, my boy, juz the man to make complete the game!' Posson Jone', it was a specious providence! I win in t'ree hours more dan six hundred dollah'! Look." He produced a mass of bank-notes, *bons*, and due-bills.

"And you got the pass?" asked the parson, regarding the money with a strange sadness.

"It is here; it take the effect so soon the daylight."

"Jools, my friend, your kindness is in vain."

The Creole's face became a perfect blank.

"Because," said the parson, "for two reasons: firstly, I have broken the laws, and ought to stand the penalty; and secondly— you must really excuse me, Jools, you know, but the pass has been got onfairly, I'm afeerd. You told the judge I was innocent; and in neither case it don't become a Christian (which I hope I can still say I am one) to 'do evil that good may come.' I muss stay."

M. St.-Ange stood up aghast, and for a moment speechless, at this exhibition of moral heroism; but an artifice was presently hit upon. "*Mais*, Posson Jone'!"—in his old *falsetto*—"de order —you cannot read it, it is in French—compel you to go h-out, sir!"

"Is that so?" cried the parson, bounding up with radiant face—"is that so, Jools?"

The young man nodded, smiling; but, though he smiled, the fountain of his tenderness was opened. He made the sign of the cross as the parson knelt in prayer, and even whispered "Hail Mary," etc., quite through, twice over.

Morning broke in summer glory upon a cluster of villas behind the city, nestled un-under live-oaks and magnolias on the banks of a deep bayou, and known as Suburb St. Jean.

With the first beam came the West-Floridian and the Creole out upon the bank below the village. Upon the parson's arm hung a pair of antique saddle-bags. Baptiste limped wearily behind; both his eyes were encircled with broad blue rings, and one cheek-bone bore the official impress of every knuckle of Colossus's left hand. The "beautiful to take care of somebody" had lost his charge. At mention of the negro he became wild, and, half in English, half in the "gumbo" dialect, said murderous things. Intimidated by Jules to calmness, he became able to speak confidently on one point; he could, would, and did swear that Colossus had gone home to the Florida parishes; he was almost certain; in fact, he thought so.

There was a clicking of pulleys as the three appeared upon the bayou's margin, and Baptiste pointed out, in the deep shadow of a great oak, the *Isabella*, moored among the bulrushes, and just spreading her sails for departure. Moving down to where she lay, the parson and his friend paused on the bank, loath to say farewell.

"O Jools!" said the parson, "supposin' Colossus ain't gone home! O Jools, if you'll look him out for me, I'll never forget you— I'll never forget you, nohow, Jools. No, Jools, I never will believe he taken that money. Yes, I know all niggahs will steal" —he set foot upon the gang-plank—"but Colossus wouldn't steal from me. Good-by."

"Misty Posson Jone'," said St.-Ange, putting his hand on the parson's arm with genuine affection, "hol' on. You see dis money—w'at I win las' night? Well, I win it by a specious providence, ain't it?"

"There's no tellin'," said the humbled Jones. "Providence

'Moves in a mysterious way
His wonders to perform.'"

"Ah!" cried the Creole, "*c'est* very true. I ged dis money in the mysterieuze way.

Mais, if I keep dis money, you know where it goin' be to-night?"

"I really can't say," replied the parson.

"Goin' to the dev'," said the sweetly smiling young man.

The schooner captain, leaning against the shrouds, and even Baptiste, laughed outright.

"O Jools, you mustn't!"

"Well, den, w'at I shall do wid *it?*"

"Any thing!" answered the parson; "better donate it away to some poor man——"

"Ah! Misty Posson Jone', dat is w'at I want. You los' five hondred dollah'—'twas my fault."

"No, it wa'n't, Jools."

"*Mais*, it was!"

"No!"

"It *was* my fault! I *swear* it was my fault! *Mais*, here is five hondred dollah';

I wish you shall take it. Here! I don't got no use for money.—Oh, my faith! Posson Jone', you must not begin to cry some more."

Parson Jones was choked with tears. When he found voice he said:

"O Jools, Jools, Jools! my pore, noble, dear, misguidened friend! ef you hed of hed a Christian raisin'! May the Lord show you your errors, better'n I kin, and bless you for your good intentions—oh, no! I cayn't touch that money with a ten-foot pole; it wa'n't rightly got; you must really excuse me, my dear friend, but I cayn't touch it."

St.-Ange was petrified.

"Good-by, dear Jools," continued the parson. "I'm in the Lord's haynds, and he's very merciful, which I hope and trust you'll find it out. Good-by!"—the schooner swung slowly off before the breeze—"good-by!"

St.-Ange roused himself.

"Posson Jone'! make me hany'ow *dis* promise: you never, never, *never* will come back to New Orleans."

"Ah, Jools, the Lord willin', I'll never leave home again!"

"All right!" cried the Creole; "I thing He's willin'. Adieu, Posson Jone'. My faith'! you are the so fighting an' moz rilligious man as I never saw! Adieu! Adieu!"

Baptiste uttered a cry and presently ran by his master toward the schooner, his hands full of clods.

St.-Ange looked just in time to see the sable form of Colossus of Rhodes emerge from the vessel's hold, and the pastor of Smyrna and Bethesda seize him in his embrace.

"O Colossus! you outlandish old niggah! Thank the Lord! Thank the Lord!"

The little Creole almost wept. He ran down the tow-path, laughing and swearing, and making confused allusion to the entire *personnel* and furniture of the lower regions.

By odd fortune, at the moment that St.-Ange further demonstrated his delight by tripping his mulatto into a bog, the schooner came brushing along the reedy bank with a graceful curve, the sails flapped, and the crew fell to poling her slowly along.

Parson Jones was on the deck, kneeling once more in prayer. His hat had fallen before him; behind him knelt his slave. In thundering tones he was confessing himself "a plumb fool," from whom "the conceit had been jolted out," and who had been made to see that even his "nigger had the longest head of the two."

Colossus clasped his hands and groaned.

The parson prayed for a contrite heart.

"Oh, yes!" cried Colossus.

The master acknowledged countless mercies.

"Dat's so!" cried the slave.

The master prayed that they might still be "piled on."

"Glory!" cried the black man, clapping his hands; "pile on!"

"An' now," continued the parson, "bring this pore, backslidin' jackace of a parson and this pore ole fool niggah back to thar home in peace!"

"Pray fo' de money!" called Colossus.

But the parson prayed for Jules.

"Pray fo' de *money!*" repeated the negro.

"And oh, give thy servant back that there lost money!"

"POSSON JONE'"

Colossus rose stealthily, and tiptoed by
his still shouting master. St.-Ange, the captain, the crew, gazed in silent wonder at the
strategist. Pausing but an instant over the
master's hat to grin an acknowledgment of
his beholders' speechless interest, he softly
placed in it the faithfully mourned and honestly prayed-for Smyrna fund; then, saluted
by the gesticulative, silent applause of St.-
Ange and the schooner men, he resumed his
first attitude behind his roaring master.

"Amen!" cried Colossus, meaning to
bring him to a close.

"Onworthy though I be——" cried Jones.

"*Amen!*" reiterated the negro.

"A-a-amen!" said Parson Jones.

He rose to his feet, and, stooping to take
up his hat, beheld the well-known roll. As
one stunned he gazed for a moment upon his

slave, who still knelt with clasped hands and
rolling eyeballs; but when he became aware
of the laughter and cheers that greeted him
from both deck and shore, he lifted eyes and
hands to heaven, and cried like the veriest
babe. And when he looked at the roll again,
and hugged and kissed it, St.-Ange tried to
raise a second shout, but choked, and the
crew fell to their poles.

And now up runs Baptiste, covered with
slime, and prepares to cast his projectiles.
The first one fell wide of the mark; the
schooner swung round into a long reach of
water, where the breeze was in her favor;
another shout of laughter drowned the male-
dictions of the muddy man; the sails filled;
Colossus of Rhodes, smiling and bowing as
hero of the moment, ducked as the main
boom swept round, and the schooner, lean-

[70]

Colossus rose stealthily and tiptoed by his still shouting
master

ing slightly to the pleasant influence, rustled a moment over the bulrushes, and then sped far away down the rippling bayou.

M. Jules St.-Ange stood long, gazing at the receding vessel as it now disappeared, now reappeared beyond the tops of the high undergrowth; but, when an arm of the forest hid it finally from sight, he turned townward, followed by that fagged-out spaniel, his servant, saying, as he turned, "Baptiste."

"*Miché?*"

"You know w'at I goin' do wid dis money?"

"*Non, miché.*"

"Well, you can strike me dead if I don't goin' to pay hall my debts! *Allons!*"

He began a merry little song to the effect that his sweetheart was a wine-bottle, and

[71]

master and man, leaving care behind, returned to the picturesque Rue Royale. The
ways of Providence are indeed strange. In
all Parson Jones's after life, amid the many
painful reminiscences of his visit to the City
of the Plain, the sweet knowledge was with-
held from him that by the light of the Christian virtue that shone from him even in his
great fall, Jules St.-Ange arose, and went to
his father an honest man.

*Swelled for a fitting retort from a
Creole gentleman*

PÈRE RAPHAËL

WHEN Jules St.-Ange said to Parson Jones in the calaboose, "M. De Blanc, he is the judge," he—abridged. The judge was M. Réné De Blanc St.-Ange—his father.

The St.-Ange house stood on the swamp side of the Rue Royale, next to a corner of that very intersection with Conti Street where Jones and Jules first met. It opened on the sidewalk and had at its ground floor, extending from the street-door steps on its right to the porte-cochère on the left, a narrow, hooded balcony masked by a lattice along its sidewalk face and across its porte-cochère end. In the great batten gate of the porte-cochère was the usual small one for servants, and close to it, in the balcony lattice, a very small hinged window. Into this balcony let also the long French windows of the drawing-room. Its unlatticed end, by the front door, was fair with potted flowers, and through the railing there one might pass to the steps and the street.

The adjoining edifice on the right, at the corner, was a prim affair of whose sort one was a great plenty—a gambling-house. Happily its main entrance was on its broader face, around in Conti Street, where it called itself a theatre. Let us not be intolerant; in the judge's own house there was lively card-playing every evening, and few could surpass the brilliancy of his own betting.

"What harm is that betting," asked the judge, "if the game is fair? In one's own domiceel, with fran'," (friends,) "ah! think!

out of what mischieve it may keeb them— on Sonday evenings!" The judge, his family of three, and even the servants were more or less addicted to what they believed was the English tongue. "Lang-uage of the law and those court'," he affably apologized, "and sinze appointed on the bench 'tis biccome one of my bad 'abit'."

He had long been a widower, the executive head of his house was his maiden sister, and both facts may, in part, explain the further one that his son was already a bitter disappointment. This very afternoon father and son had quarrelled and the son had been forbidden the house. Florestine, youngest of the household, was really not a relative, but the orphan of the judge's old law partner. She was as beautiful and intelligent as she was high-spirited, and the judge doted on high spirit. His last hope for his son lay in the young man's invincible mettle.

Within an hour after the rupture there came to the house those "only two really dear and good Américaines in the worl',— although Protestan', alas!" — the widow Merrifield and her mild blue-eyed daughter Abigail. Mrs. Merrifield's call was not merely social; she had a matter in hand which she could not with comfort carry directly to the widower judge, albeit he was an old friend and her lawyer; yet it was a matter in which, through his sister, she *must* seek his kind offices. For it was one in which only a Creole gentleman could know how to intervene, and she had already made bold to refer to him M. Dimitry Davezac, another and much younger Creole gentleman. Had he called? No? She was glad.

Yes, the matter was about Abby, and when the mother had stated it to Mademoiselle St.-Ange—while Florestine had led Abigail up-stairs to a conversation quite as private and far more intense—and the judge's sister came back from the judge's part of the house and from telling him the Davezac case, the widow's heart was lighter.

And now she and Abby must fly, night was so near. But a coming storm thundered No! and mademoiselle calmed them with the assurance that after the rain Florestine's maid Caroline, with one of the men-servants, should conduct them home, since the judge could not.

"On account those sore h-eye'," he explained with gallant regret, touching the green pasteboard shade which overhung his brows. "But, any'ow," he said, "that pain

of the light is now nearly pass'. Thangs be
to God, those sigs week' to wear me that
accursed thing, they finizh on the day after
to-morrow; then 'tis my 'ope to 'ave the
more smooth tamper."

The five were yet standing together when
the rain began to fall, and Caroline ushered
in kind old Father Pierre, taking refuge from
the weather. Good company he was, and an
hour passed brightly while all tongues ran
nimbly, and five hearts, not counting his, hid
each its own distress. A second hour followed, and then, in a lull of the tremendous
rain, the good priest, laughing away the
judge's protest, rose to go. The Merrifields
openly admired his masculine ability to
pooh-pooh the "must not" of a friend.

As the two men stepped out into the shel-
tered balcony the judge had new wrenchings

of secret torture to think of his son out in this tempest with no better comfort than the companionship of that mulatto scamp Baptiste—Caroline's lover, by the way. All at once, hardly knowing what he did, he told the bare fact of the quarrel and then as abruptly changed the subject. "But, my faith! how that Florestine has been to me an angel those sigs week' of those sore h-eye'! Had it not 'ave been for that Florestine I muz' 'ave suffer' those sigs week' without one game of card'."

Caroline stood at close earshot just there in the porte-cochère wicket, where she had come to catch any stray news there might be of her momselle Florestine's beloved Jules and her own "triflin'" Baptiste, and she heard even Father Pierre's soft words.

"My fran'," said he after a moment of

meditation, "you muz' not priv-ent yo' son to make that h-angel yo' daughter."

Caroline, in a wild gladness, listened on. "Ah!" exclaimed the judge, "my son *he* muz' not priv-ent *me* to make her my daughter. You know well I have swear that to her father; but also I have swear him that my son shall not know that till he get her, and he shall not have her till he is fit!"

"Fit? Ah, well, when tha' 'z going to be?"

"Father Pierre, you preach againz' those seven sin, eh? You are a pries', you got to do that. Me, I preach only againz' one; that is—debt! When my son pay h-all his debt' he can have Florestine; but biffo'? he shall not even h-ask for her."

"Ah! but ad the same time, so soon he *say*——"

"No; only so soon he *pay!*"

"Yes; but I thing if you let me *tell* him he can have her so soon he pay——"

"No-o! When he have *pay*—that laz' dolla'—*I* will tell him *if* he can have her or no. But he—you know what he say? He tell me—when I be ready to say he can have her, *then* he let me know if he goin' pay *any* of those debt'."

"But if he 'ave no money——"

"Let him go to work, sacré tonn'—pardon! He shall not one dollah risceive from me till he pay his debt', not to save the life! Well, good-night—biffo' it rain hard some mo'—Father Pierre, a moment! I am no miser, me—no! That *hour* my son is finizh' to pay those debt', I swear you, I give him back aggain two dollah for one, every dollah he have pay. Only tha' 'z another thing he muz' not know biffo'. Well, good-night!"

PÈRE RAPHAËL

The judge watched his friend hurry away through the wet lamplight. The skies poured again, and he from the balcony—Caroline from the wicket—fled into the house. There the Merrifields were bowing to the decree of mademoiselle and Florestine that they must stay all night. Who could argue against such a pair backed by such a sky? While they asked the door-bell rang, and with their hostess they started for their rooms; but Florestine untwined her arms from Abigail, laid them on her guardian's neck, and offered to stay with him and once more be his eyes. The other three hurried on up-stairs and M. Davezac entered.

How the storm-delayed suitor had contrived, after all, to arrive so nearly dry was remarkable, only his feet being wet enough to justify his neglect of an invitation to be

seated. Manifestly he was from the country
—the sugar country—and as haughty as he
was handsome. His dress was odd, even for
New Orleans. He wore buckskin breeches
above his exquisite top-boots, and a fawn-
skin vest under his voluminous coat, giving
an effect half pioneer, half Incroyable. To
Florestine, as she sat close to her guardian's ear, he seemed, save Jules, as fair a
youth as she had ever looked upon. The
judge explained her presence and his dis-
figuring green shade, and at once came to
business.

"Madame Merrifiel' she say you come
tell her you every day passin' at Place Congo,
by her house, see her daughter up on bal-
conie, and fall in love to her till you cann'
stan' that no mo', and you want madame let
you come make visite."

The youth bowed grandly: "Tha' 'z w'at I want."

"Yes. Well, tha' 'z maybee h-all right, if you got some fran' want to speak good word for you."

"No, m'sieu'." The lover stiffened up till he could but just peer down over his lower lashes: "h-all those fran' livin' on planta-tion'."

But the judge, still wrung with the pain of having parted two lovers, had no inclina-tion to part another two. "Tha' 'z an un-fortunate," he said. "Any'ow, me, I bil-ieve you one gen'leman, though I'm not ab'e to see you, bic-ause those sore h-eye'. That be pretty good, if you get fran' on plantation' send sairtifi-*cate*."

The young man stood with chin lifted and eyes dropped. "M'sieu', I bet you

w'at you want; I swear you w'at you want;
I fight you who you want; but sairtifi-*cate?*
—bah!"

"But sit down. I bil-ieve I like you pretty
good. Me, I don' want you to bet, neither
to fight; only I like you to swear me one
thing the truth."

The petitioner somewhat relaxed: "Verie
well, m'sieu'; I swear you the truth, I don'
care w'at it is."

"Verie well. You h-owe some debt', I
sue-pose; 'ow much you h-owe?"

The youth showed a faint smile of scorn.
"Not one dollah," he said, and hardened his
neck as he added, "even to my papa."
Catching signs of approval from Florestine,
he condescended further: " 'Tis to ezcape
that that I am from home. I could 'ave res'
yond' so long I want. I am a Davezac!"

He curved back until he had to lean on his cane. Florestine whispered some suggestion to the judge, who murmured his approval of it.

"'Sieur Davezac," he said, "you don't got one father *con*-fessor?""

"Yes," replied the suitor; but when he discerned Florestine's wish that he would show himself more compliant, he added: "Yes, m'sieu', tha' 'z Père Raphaël. I shall send you Père Raphaël?"

"Père—eh—Raphaël—eh?" mused the judge. "Ah, I dunno; I thing I'm maybee not verie well acquain'd with that father. He's a verie h-old, that Père Raphaël?"

The young man darkened; he suspected a sly attempt at cross-examination. "No, m'sieu'; that Père Raphaël he's a verie yo'ng."

"Ah, yes; a verie yo'ng, yes; but is he not a verie large fat ?"

M. Davezac bridled. "No, m'sieu'; he's a verie small thin."

The judge seemed all at once to remember: "Ah, yes! But—exceb' the hand' and feet, eh ?"

The reply came with a smile as sweet as Florestine's, yet distinctly threatening: "No, m'sieu'; hand' and feet same size my ear', and I 'ope my inquisitor he don't find those the ear' of a jack-*ass* ?"

Florestine colored in protest, but the judge laughed outright. "Ah, no-o! Send me that Père Raphaël. If I like him so well I like you, that be h-all right."

At a pause in the storm the visitor bowed himself out. The judge went to his room, Florestine mounted to hers. There she

learned from Caroline the glorious things
overheard at the porte-cochère wicket, and
between her distress for the storm-beaten
Jules and her vivid and highly practical
plannings to make use of her dear guardian's incautious revelations, she slept as
little, all night, as the judge or his sister or
Madame Merrifield

The Sabbath began to dawn, the rain-
spent clouds to break, and Florestine, for the
hundredth time, looked down into the
drenched and still lamplighted street. Her
mind revolved an astounding plot she had
laid while others slept. She was seeking its
moral justification.

"To the gayest endurance," thought she,
"there is a limit. People have no right to
forget that. The judge has no right. No

more has dear Tante"—as she called
mademoiselle St.-Ange. "Yet only Caroline
remembers—ah, faithful Caroline! But
where is *she* presently, that frightful lag-
gard?" The sufferer tearfully smiled.

She lingered at the open casement, taking
comfort in the triumphant rearising of the
storm-swept city. Remotely she could hear
the shock-headed Gascons of the French
Market whistling and singing and making
its vaults resound with the ring of their busy
cleavers.

"How happy," she sighed, "is the lot of
the butcher!"

A watchman, with lantern and leather
helmet, came up the street and gave three
slowly swung taps of his iron-shod club on
the corner curbstone as a signal to his fel-
lows. "What a care-free life is that of the

watchman!—as, likewise,"—her contempla-
tion taking in a two-wheeled milk-cart and
a two-wheeled bread-cart wildly tilted in the
mire, stalled and abandoned—"as likewise
the life of the milkman and the baker!"

The carts stood under a lamp which, from
a great crane, overhung the two ways. An
hour earlier she had seen them crash together, and it had been balm to her soul's
wounds to hear their drivers exchange the
compliments customary on such occasions.
"What splandid liberties are to the milkman, the bread man—while to the gayest
and moze girlish enduranze there is a limit!"

A lamplighter passed, quenching the
lamps: "'Ow 'appy is the lot of the lamplighter!"

Day broadened; one could read a distant
poster that promised amazing things for

PÈRE RAPHAËL

Cayetano's Circus on the Place Congo. The shops began to open, yonder pawnshop down street on the farther side not excepted. Men and women, white, black, yellow, passed with market-baskets on arm, and here came a slave maid as straight as an Egyptian and as black as Creole coffee, with a huge basket, heaping full, on her head. At the porte-cochère a milkman sent in his usual catcall, and the wicket latch clinked. That was Caroline with her pitcher.

Florestine saw the departing milkman turn the upper street corner, but heard no wicket reclosed: "Ah, Caroline, murderess!" she inwardly cried, "do you want to bring yo' miztrezz ad the door of death, standing idle, doubtlezz, down there in the 'alf-open wicket?"

She did not guess that Baptiste had come

upon the scene, nor could she hear any note
of Caroline's wary speech: "No, suh! no
milk fo' you tell you go an' come ag'in; an'
no mo' sweet-sweetenin' o' dis yeh gal tell
she know who gwine marry her missy! By
de law I goes wid my missy, thaynk Gawd!
an' I don' go sweetheartenin' wid no French
yalleh niggah to-day to be his grass-widdeh
to-morrow! No, suh; you go ten times fas-
teh 'n you come, an' fetch me yo' mawsteh!"

A bread man filled the maid's arms with
loaves and hurried on. She gave one to the
mulatto. "Here, pig; now fo' de Lawd's
sake, run on an'——"

"Yass, yass; but, Caroline, y' ought to
see! All behine Rue Bourgogne h-overflow'!"

"Lawd 'a' massy! man, I wants to see
Miché Jules! I got dat news fo' Miché Jules,
what——"

PÈRE RAPHAËL

The messenger went, but Abigail Merrifield, slipping down through the drawing-room and out into the latticed balcony, heard Caroline moan after him, to see him stop and share his loaf with a very black and rustic old negro who presently moved on with him out of sight. With the wicket shut Abigail breathed easier, though still in a tremor of hope, longing, and self-blame.

She was just in time. Dimitry Davezac came up the far side of the street with the high-minded air of a man who could always be counted on. As he passed, as he glanced across at all the upper balconies of the house, and as he looked back while he turned riverward into the Rue Conti, Abigail, in the lattice, as badly frightened as she was well hid, stood as still as a stone. Her heart pounded like a ship on a reef—it was a ship

on a reef! Oh, what would her mother say
if she knew her child had not the self-command, the moral force, even to retreat into
the house? The question gave her strength
to start, but at that moment some one entered
the drawing-room and she could only stand
petrified again.

Around in the Rue Conti the young man's
steps flagged—flagged—ceased. He laid
the head of his cane to his lips. Then he
pressed smartly on again. This was but
for a moment, however, and his trim feet
went slowly once more. He stopped,
turned half round, looked back, consulted
his watch, frowned. All pure stage-play;
he was recollecting nothing which he had
left behind and must return for; yet now he
went back. At the same time Abigail was
having great relief from her fears. Who-

ever had come into the drawing-room, she
thought, must have gone out again, it was
so still. Here at hand offered itself, more-
over, a plausible task, and with healing
caresses she began to reanimate the storm-
torn flowers at the open end of the balcony.
Now she soothed this one and now that, and
this, and this, and this; reaching, bending,
drawing back, half straightening, and bending again, a languid flower herself, while
Dimitry came once more into view and
moved down the farther sidewalk.

"What odd chimneys and dormer-win-
dows!" his manner implied, and she saw
him even when he had got entirely at her
back. Ah, but she should have seen more!
The very flowers, laughing through their
grateful tears, tried to cry, "Look behind
you, benefactress! Look, Abigail, behind

you in the balcony!" For who had unlaw-
fully slipped into this show and was seeing
the whole performance free but Florestine!

Davezac was gone, yet Abby's touch lingered among the flowers, and not until a
voice as soft as their perfume called her name
did she flash round to stare and gasp. Sud-
donly her tears shone and she clung to the
arm of her friend. "I couldn't sleep. I
couldn't keep my room."

"Ah, tha' 'z not the fault of you. Tha' 'z
the fault of Tante to give you that room
behine yo' mama, and withoud balconie-e!"

"Oh, Florestine, this is the first time in
my life I ever——"

"Did anything! Ah, ha, ha! I billieve
you, Abbee; I billieve that, my faith!"

"Oh, oh! If you could only have told me
last night what took place between the judge

and—and *him*, I might now be honestly asleep."

"Ah, I cou'n' he'p *that*. I had to keep me with the judge till the en', biccause those sore h-eye'. Then, after, I cou'n' come to you in that room behine. I can tell you now, but I don't want tell you if that goin' put you as-leep."

But Abigail begged and Florestine told.

As she finished—"Oh, Florestine, Florestine," cried her listener, "you've made his heart's fortune—his and mine together!"

"Attendez—wait; tha' 'z not sure yet. We dunno if that Père Raphaël—of the so small han' an' feet, ha, ha!—be willing to come. And even if he come we dunno if the judge goin' be please' with Père Raphaël."

"Oh, but he will, he will. Ah, darling, how can I ever repay you?"

[99]

PÈRE RAPHAËL

"You want to know? Come! Come inside! You can pay in advanze." They hastened to Florestine's chamber, where Florestine explained. "You shall make 'Sieur Davezac take me this letter to Jules." She showed one. "Ah, Abbee, 'ow glad the good God muz' be, now, that he led them teach me to write! But firz' I'll tell you w'at Caroline fine out laz' night from the judge."

While she recounted the entrancing story, Jules St.-Ange, with Baptiste at his back, stood on the sidewalk close by his lost home. To this outcast pair the inundation had made the shape of the earth newly problematical. Baptiste was perplexed, but his master, as ever, remained cheerful and unbiassed. "Me, I dunno," he said "but I thing it is roun', mais ad the same time flat—

like a plate. Because, me, if I was making
that worl' I would try to suit every-*bodie*,
and I thing that muz' be the way 'tis make.
You fine it flat; well, then, it is flat: Father
Pierre fine it roun'; well, then, it is roun'
—mais that Caroline!—wanting to see me so
bad—w'ere she is hide?"

"Ah, I dunno; laz' time she was righd
there. I shall knock?"

"Knock? ad the porte-cochère of my
papa? Baptiste, 'f you knock there I sell
you to-day, h-auction! Knock if you want;
that h-auction raise me some money for the
bread and coffee, else, me, I dunno 'ow I'm
goin' raise that."

While he spoke M. St.-Ange noted with
mingled amusement and regard, on the other
side of the way, a strikingly dressed stranger.
It was Davezac, passing again, and the two

gave each other stare for stare. The spying maidens, from Florestine's high chamber, could see Dimitry, though not Jules.

"Sacré!" murmured the lover of Abigail between his perfect teeth, "any plaze but there, and with her perchanze looking, I would crozz all that mud and make you to elucidade that stare; but I'll see you aggain."

He scanned him sidewise, carefully; so much too carefully that, to Florestine's exquisite entertainment, he ran into a towering backwoodsman, who affectionately apologized, while street observers and even the frightened Abigail laughed; but Jules so courteously refrained that M. Davezac forgave his earlier offence.

Up on the next square Dimitry looked back. At the corner opposite the front of the judge's house people were running to-

gether from all directions. Bareheaded in
the midst of the press towered the backwoodsman, Parson Jones. Presently he
was talking to Jules, who had crossed to his
side. However, two or three onlookers from
upper balconies said it was all a false alarm,
and as they spoke Dimitry espied Caroline
slip from her wicket and hurry his way,
though with the street between them. Now
she sidled into an arch, openly smiled at him,
and slyly showed Florestine's letter. He
went to her swiftly enough, read and parleyed; parleyed twice as long as he would
have done had he known that Abigail was
once more in the lattice.

"But, oh, Florestine," said the over-
matched Abby—for Florestine was with her
and had revealed her whole mad plot, pro-
posing to make it a round conspiracy of five,

including Caroline—"that would be to steal! to steal, Florestine! How can I—can I—ask him to help me steal?"

"Ste-eal! Ah, ha, ha, Abbee, you dunno bittween to steal and to borrow?"

"Oh, but to strip the house like a gang of thieves—ah, me, me! It's tearing my poor conscience in two!"

"Abbee, look!" Florestine counted off on her fingers: "Firs', we take all those bric-à-brac; segond, 'Sieur Davezac he pawn them yondeh and give the money to Jules; three, Jules he pay with it all his debt'; four, the judge he give aggain to Jules the double all he pay; five, we rid-deem those bric-à-brac, and the fortune of the 'eart is make for every-*bodie*. Ah, Abbee, if you don't help me to make that, you tear my poor conscien' in fi-i-ive!"

"Oh, sweet, I am such an awful coward!"

"Ah, yes, but sometime' they are very uzeful, those coward'."

"But you spoke of difficulties——"

"Yes, ah, yes! Firz' place, I dunno can we make Jules take those money, he is a so proud of his honor! And, segond place, ev'n if he do that, I dunno if he h-use those money to pay those debt'—ha, ha, ha! *Than* w'at we goin' do, w'en Tante and the judge big-in to mizz those candelabra, those vase', those spoo-oon'?"

Abigail gasped and moaned, but Florestine clutched her arm and they peered through the lattice. Up their own sidewalk came Parson Jones, and at his elbow tripped Jules St.-Ange. The parson was making reckless show of his bank-notes, which Jules regarded with lively desire while he warned their holder of his folly. Behind the two were Baptiste and Colossus, with the loaf they had shared stowed safely inside them. The four passed close by the lattice. Florestine, gathering some hint of Jules's design, sent him a soft call of distress, but Parson Jones drowned it unaware with the re-echoing voice in which he explained that the fund belonged to his church in the wilderness, and invited Jules to breakfast.

"Abbee, Abbee," she gasped, "I shall follow them!"

But Abby seized her as if the pair were drowning together, and in panting suspense Florestine lingered and gazed. The gambling-house! the gambling-house at the corner! Would Jules lead the stranger into it? For there the two masters and servants had halted. But the maidens took courage

Florestine . . . sent him a soft call of distress

when they heard the parson set forth his theory of a special Providence, and Jules profess a like conviction. And now grateful ears sprang into Florestine's eyes as the men turned away, picked their steps across the mire of the Rue Royale, and disappeared toward the Rue Chartres.

"Wait, darling, wait!" whispered the clinging Abigail. "There's hope yet; let me think a moment!"

"Ah!" cried the more daring one, "sinze all night I have wait and think. Watch you there; I goin' fedge those bric-à-brac!" She darted in.

Abigail wrung her hands. "I cannot do this!" she cried, "I cannot, I cannot!" Yet where courage failed, friendship held fast, and her act was stouter than her word. She flinched with affright, for Caroline, who had returned unnoticed, softly called in through the lattice from the angle by the porte-cochère.

"I foun' him, Miss Abbie, yass 'm. But, well, eh, he say Père Raphaël ain't comin'. Don't give no reason, he say, 'cep' dat Miché Dabzac he stay away too much f'om confession."

"W'at, w'at, w'at?" exclaimed Florestine, as she reappeared with a small heavy burden wrapped in a large woollen garment.

"Oh, Lawdy, missy," said the maid, " Père Raphaël refuse' to come!"

Caroline!" The mistress snatched open the lattice window. "Assassin, you! 'Sieur Davezac—*he* riffuse to come, al-*so?*"

"Lawd, no! He waitin' dess round de cawneh; but he 'fraid nobody gwine trus' him now sence Père Raphaël 'fuse to come."

"Go, Caroline, slow torture, you! fly! Tell him come! Tell him Père Raphaël he 'ave change' his mind!"

"Florestine!" gasped Abigail.

"Mais certainement! Caroline, tell him Père Raphaël sen' the judge word he comin' speak well-well for him. Allez! va!"

The maid glided away. Her mistress set down her burden and, drawing the wrapper from it, whispered, "Hun'rade-dolla' clock to big-in!"

Abigail gulped. "In the judge's own cloak!" she moaned.

"Ah, no," replied her smiling friend; "and, any'ow, we don't goin' to pawnbreak *that*. But you, Abbee; you di'n' prayed laz' night for Père Raphaël to come?"

"I had never heard of Père Raphaël!"

"Ah, yes; you never hear'; and yet ad

the same time you di'n' billieve he's coming! Ah, Abbee, I dunno 'ow you can be a so wicked like that! Mais wait there whiles I fedge some more of those thing'."

The next moment Abigail, left alone, saw Dimitry reappear at the corner. Caroline was with him, but they parted; she came, he went in search of Jules. He turned the corner St.-Ange and the parson had turned; but unluckily he had not seen them enter the parson's lodging-house, and thinking they had passed on into and down the Rue Chartres, he hastened that way.

"Oh, yass 'm," said Caroline, again at the lattice window, "he be right back. He on'y gwine tell Miché Jules fo' Gawd's sake don't go gitt'n' money in no scan'lous way whiles we a-raisin' it faw him squah and clean."

"Abbee!" cried Florestine, returning with fresh booty, "'ow you are fine, to be a so brave like that, an' same time withoud a teaspoon of courage!"

"I think so, myself!" was the flashing reply.

When the breakfast-bell tinkled and Florestine, busy as a bird with nestlings, caught her breath and hearkened, fortune was kind. Mrs. Merrifield, Tante, and the judge, worn with the cares of a sleepless night, sent excuses for their non-appearance. So prospered the reckless scheme, and presently, while Abigail, alone, and always the better nerved in Florestine's absence, watched in the balcony for her lover's return, there came instead, without their servants and unfound by Davezac, Jules St.-Ange and Parson Jones. Through what a maze the prodigal was leading his victim! They passed again down street and out of sight.

Laden with her final spoils Florestine stepped into the balcony once more and Abigail told of the two men. "And there's hope yet, dear," she said with spirit, "for they're on their way to church; I heard them say so. At any rate we can wait and see!"

"Wait!" replied Florestine, "for Jules to go to church? Ah, no!"

Caroline emerged from the porte-cochère and passed up through the lattice the family's biggest market-basket, and while Florestine filled it Dimitry arrived.

"Now, Miss Abby," said the maid, "please han' me dat ah big dud fo' to kyiver de load. Thank you, ma'am. Lead off, Miché Dabzac, and de Lawd have mussy on ow souls!"

[112]

"Stop! stop!" commanded Abigail, with sudden authority, "let us—oh, let us—oh, wait, wait!"

"Mademoiselle," put in her lover—he tried to show the tenderest worship, but it was the first word he had ever spoken to her and he burst into a blaze—"I break any law you want! Even I *keep* any law you want. But to wait? My God! Mademoiselle, sinze five hun'rade year' di'n' no Davezac wait for no-*body!* Allons, Caroline!"

By his aid the great load had risen to the slave girl's head, and as they went it rested there as jauntily as a flowered hat. The two maidens watched them go in at the pawn-broker's door, and were looking for them to come forth again, when all at once Flores-tine dragged Abigail from the balcony, and from a drawing-room window showed her

Tante and Mrs. Merrifield issuing into the street by the front door. "Tsh-sh! they thing we are there in my room asleep together; Caroline tole that to them w'en yo' mama di'n' fine you in yo' bed. Ah, yo' mama she 'ave her li'l' sicret, too. She want to go and riturn withoud you finding that out—ha, ha, ha!—that she have been *there*."

"Where?"

"Ah! only to mass. She don't want riffuse that to Tante, an' same time she dunno if tha' 'z maybee a li'l' bit wrong, and of course, you know, the only way to fine that out 't is to try it. Then if you fine it wrong you be sorrie, and that make it right." The pair came out again into the balcony and after much anxious waiting Davezac and Caroline reappeared.

[114]

"W'at! Caroline, you 'ave the sick stomach—to smile like that?"

"Momselle, 'cept dis yeh old dud what you tell me be sho' to fetch back, do whole kit an' bilin' brung dess half what we bound to raise."

"Ah, mon Dieu! and if Tante fine those thing' gone!"

"Mesdemoiselles," interposed Dimitry, "look! I shall go at my room—bring h'all my thing'—raise that balanze in half an hour!"

"Whiles they are at mass!" broke in the delighted Florestine. "Yass! 'Tis the h-only way, Abbee. Go, 'Sieur Davezac, go. God will pay you for that! Go, make quick biffo' Père Raphaël come fine uz all here together. Go! and same time send me that Jules St.-Ange, while me I make Père Raph-

aël tell the judge you makin' yo' possible to
bring him back his son."

A half-hour was all that remained of the
Sabbath forenoon, and Judge St.-Ange had
not yet left his bedchamber, when the front-
door bell rang and Caroline went up-stairs
to announce Père Raphaël.

"Yass, suh, an' he got"—she made a dis-
tressed effort not to smile at thought of the
two figures meeting—"he got a green shade
ove' his eyes biggeh 'n yone."

Père Raphaël paced the drawing-room
alone, truly "a verie small thin." The house
was still. Now and again as the scant form,
trim even in the rude draping of rope-tied
gown and unlifted cowl, came to the balcony
windows, the deeply hooded eyes looked
out, first down the street and then up. Thus

they were presently drawn to a number of unwashed little girls near the next door, a door of the gambling-house. The flock were listening against it, giggling, trying to peep under it, starting away, wringing hands, and stealing back to listen again. Père Raphaël stepped out upon the open end of the balcony.

"'Tis Miché Jules," said a brazen young-ster, her eyes on the green shade, her apron in her teeth. "Yass, he pass in yondeh wid a so beeg man, by front way, round cawneh, and beeg man he don't want play card', and he yell so loud dey scared of him."

The visitor returned to the drawing-room, wearily chose a chair and knelt beside it, but instantly stood upright again at sound of a footfall.

Judge St.-Ange came slowly in and paused. "Caroline!" he called. The maid came.

"Mademoiselle Florestine," he asked, "where she is?"

"Miché, she say Miss Abby got sich a pow'ful migraine she feel bound to stay wid her ef you kin escuse her; yass, suh."

The judge waved out the servant and turned to his visitor. Père Raphaël's eyes remained downcast behind their ugly screen until the two were seated.

"Is that a fact, indeed," asked the judge, "that we 'ave the one maladie?"

"Ah," replied the little father, in a thin, obstructed voice, "with me 'tis but a cold, and in the throat like-*wise*, till I was nearly privvent the honor to come."

"They privvent many thing', those sore h-eye'," agreed the judge.

"Yes," rejoined the caller, "I cannot read me those prayer', cannot wride me those sermon'. Almoze they stop me playing those domino'—those card'."

"Ha-a-ah! you are fon' of those card'?"

"Yes, I am verie, verie fon' to play them. Mais, w'en I cann' play, that save me money. Biccause those hoss-raze—those cock-*fight* —I never bet on *those*. Tha' 'z only thing I ever bet, me,—those card'."

"And me the same," said the judge. A business silence ensued. Then—"Père Raphaël, that young man—he is one of those Davezac', I sue-pose, of the Côte d'Or, eh? You can speak good word for him?"

"Ah, that dippan'. Me, I h-am a pries'; you, you h-are a judge. I dunno w'at goin' be good word to *you*. 'Sieur Davezac he got, h-any'ow, all the bad 'abit' nécessaire to a perfec' Creole gen'leman."

"Aha! Well, tha' 'z mighty good word.

[119]

For one pries' tha'd be verie bad; but for one Creole gen'leman, you know——"

"Hmm. Mais, same time, there is one diffycultie, m'sieu'."

"Tha' 'z not mannie."

"Mais, I thing that don't please you, m'sieu'. I 'ave the fear that Madame Merrifiel' she 'ave the 'ope that M. Davezac he 'ave the willingnezz to change his *ril*-igion. Mais, I am compel to tell you—w'at he tell me—rather than change his *ril*-igion he sooner go to hell. Pardon, I am sorrie to tell you that, mais—" The small speaker shrugged from ears to elbows.

The host hid his admiration under a cold smile. "Tha' 'z brave, yes," he acknowledged.

"Brave—ah, tha' 'z another troub'—h-all the time fightingg, fightingg, or fran' of somebody fightingg!"

"Ah! but a gen'leman, those time'—! My faith! Père Raphaël, he shall 'ave everything w'at he want. For why he did'n' come with you?"

"M'sieu', he is af-raid to be in debt to you."

"'Ow he's goin' be in debt to me? Impossib'!"

"He say if you speak well for him to Madame Merrifiel' he is in debt to you the res' of the life, and he don't want see you aggain till any'ow he *commance* to pay you, and he's gone pawnbroken everything w'at he got——"

"Ah!—ah-h!—ah-h-h! My fran', oh-h, w'at that is for?"

"M'sieu', 'tis for—pardon, to tell you that, 'tis a diffycult; tha' 'z a verie daily-cat."

With his eyes helplessly dropped, the

host straightened severely against the high back of his chair. "'Tis ab-out my son? Ah—go h-on."

"Well, you see, 'Sieur Davezac he hearin' every-*bodie* talk 'bout *that*. And w'en he say he bet any-*bodie*—fight any-*bodie*—w'at say Judge St.-Ange he don't trit his son all right, then every-*bodie* say, 'Oh, yes; the judge he *thing* he trit his son all right, mais if the judge know that ris-on his son don't pay those debt'——'"

"Ris-on he don't pay—he don't want!"

"Yes; mais they thing 'tis bic-ause yo' son he's fran' of so many poor man, and every time one poor fran' cann' pay his debt' yo' son he pay that with his h-own monie."

The judge shook his drooping head mournfully. "I do not bil-ieve. I never

fine one sign of that. If I 'ave see' that, my
son he would sleep laz' night in his h-own
bed, and me I would sleep in mine. Mon
Dieu! Père Raphaël, tha' 'z a thing I don'
like to talk ab-out, but—w'at I muz find out
—'ow that make 'Sieur Davezac take all his
thing' pawnshop?"

"Ah, I tell you. He say he goin' find that
Jules St.-Ange, goin' lend him those monie,
goin' *make* him pay h-all those debt'. Then
he make him go at his papa, and say, 'At the
end I 'ave *commance*' all right, I goin' to
work.'"

The judge looked up sharply, but then
sank his head lower than before. "I don't
bil-ieve th' 'z a possib' to make. Same time
already, me, I am in the debt to 'Sieur
Davezac so long my life; if he succeed to
finizh, or if he don't succeed to finizh, to me

that be h-all the same; he 'ave *commance*'. To *commance*, 'tis enough." His grip trembled on the arms of his chair, but his head came up.

"I thing tha' 'z verie well, m'sieu,' " said Père Raphaël, stirring as if to go. A strange voice was distracting both visitor and host with mad though remote and smothered bellowings. The judge, in apology said that they came from the next house, through the walls.

"I never year it loud like that biffo'. Père Raphaël, I want you tell 'Sieur Davezac—and same time my son I don't want him fine that out—if 'Sieur Davezac he succeed, my son he 'ave planty to pay him back, bic-ause me I shall give my son twice w'at he spend to pay h-all those debt'—never biffo' I di'n' year some noises come through thad wall."

"All right, m'sieu'; I tell him—if I see him. Mais, there is one thing: 'Sieur Davezac he say maybee those monie he raise be not enough to pay h-all those debt'; well, any'ow, w'en you see yo' son *commance* to pay, you be satis-*fy;* to commance, 'tis enough. Mais me, I——''

With a shrug the speaker rose, and the judge stood up very straight.

"Père Raphaël, no; tha' 'z all w'at I can say—no! For 'Sieur Davezac to commance *'tis* enough, yes; but for my son—and still, my God! with my son I be glad be recon-*cile'* —for him to commance, 'tis too late; he muz' finizh." The speaker's tone, though grieved, was kind, and the raising of his voice was solely to divert his visitor from the noises that continued to search through the partition wall. "Come at home

here aggain this evening, will you? If that
troub' with my son pass, or if it be worse,
all the same I be wanting you bad—fellow-
sufferer those sore h-eye'—to play me some
card'."

The visitor promised to come, and bowed
low for thanks, but both were giving all
their heed to the hot altercation that searched
through the solid masonry and was bringing
the judge undisguised distress. Père Raphaël had faced toward the front door, the
judge following and trying to flood the air
with his own speech, when there came from
the gambler's house a sound as of some one
falling, and outcries in several voices. Then
there was a jangle of the St.-Ange door-bell.
The ready Caroline flew to the door, and
Madame Merrifield and Tante sprang in,
casting wild glances behind them.

"There!" cried the hostess, with a sister's indignation in every inch of her bonnet and draperies. "Lis-ten! Look! Come there and look, you! You what cannod take ad-vize! Oh, you what, sinze appointed jodge, got no time to be a father!"

The judge caught one outside glimpse and turned away with a groan. In the midst of a multiplying crowd the towering form of Parson Jones, between a burly red ruf-fian on one side and Jules St.-Ange on the other, was being hurried away, sway-ing bloody-headed, across the Rue Royale. The three men vanished into the cross street.

"He fine his money gone," cried one child to another. "Dey say one niggah take it; dey gone hunt him up!"

"Caroline, my 'at and shoe'!" exclaimed

the judge, and would have torn the shade from his eyes, but the sister prevented him. A better thought came. "Père Raphaël"— he tried to peer this way and that—"Père Raphaël, go you, tell my son—ah, my God! where is that Père Raphaël?"

"Gone already!" joyously cried Caroline. "Lef' at de fus' beginnin'!" She turned to Florestine and Abigail, who stood clinging to each other, Florestine as pale and grief-broken as though she had been Abigail, and Abigail as strangely full of a new intrepidity as if she were Florestine. "You see him go, bofe 'n you, didn' you? You didn'? He go by de po'te-cochère; yass, suh; crossin' tow'd de riveh, in Toulouse Street, like he gwine head 'em off."

"Go you, Caroline," said the judge, and Florestine spoke the same word, straighten-

"Fine, Miché Jules! Jules!"

ing from Abby's clasp. "Go, make quick!
You shall fine him!"

But as the young mistress pushed her maid
from the room, she added privately: "Fine
Miché Jules! Jules! Jules! Fine Miché
Jules!"

The judge turned to Madame Merrifield.
"Yo' pardon! 'Twas not to give you *that*
troub' that those heaven' make you our prisoner; for you I 'ave a different news." Abby
moved away, and he spoke on in a murmur.
"Père Raphaël, as you 'ave seen——"

The lady received the information with
due dignity and thanks, and presently turned
to her daughter. "Come, my dear, the over-
flow has passed off. Put on your things and
let us——"

Abigail was beseeching Tante to allow
Florestine to go home with her, and when

Madame Merrifield urged it the petition was granted.

"Here tha' 'z no place for her ad the presend," said the sister aside to her brother, with tremulous energy.

"Ah, verie good!" was his reply. "For me, I goin' make my son fine out I *am* a judge!" And the moment he was alone he rang for a man-servant and sent him on an errand that filled the slave's face with consternation.

Madame Merrifield's tall house, in which, this afternoon, she was taking some of the sleep owing to her from the night, stood flush with the sidewalk, with its garden on one side, at the corner of two streets. Through its oleanders and myrtles and its high wooden fence of graceful openwork one got a broken view of the rude Place Congo, in a part of which a great multitude were gathered on the board seats of Cayetano's amphitheatre to see his buffalo-and-tiger fight.

Abigail and Florestine were in the garden. The sounds and glimpses they caught in their embowered hiding would have yielded few clear meanings, but Caroline, outside the double gate, went and came, describing and explaining. *That?* That was the up-river men jeering at the Latins. And *that?* That was the Latins snarling back at the Américains. Oh, there would be bloody trouble if the show did not come off soon! *That?* That was the Américains singing. Yes, the tune was a hymn, the maid admitted to Abigail, "But you can dess thaynk Gawd you cayn't make out de words."

Once she came excitedly saying she had

seen, seated in the throng, at inaccessible
distances and apart, Colossus and Baptiste.
She hurried back in hope to discover Jules,
the parson, or Dimitry; but as she vanished
Dimitry came along, scanning every window
of the house, and quite overlooking the garden until Florestine stepped from cover to the
half-open gate. He strode in a step or two,
lifted his hat, and with the glow of an aide-
de-camp used it to point to the Place Congo.

"Mademoiselle, I cannot stop. I am
cloze be'ind the track of 'Sieur St.-Ange.
Some-*bodie* pig' the pocket of that Posson
Jone', and Posson Jone' and 'Sieur St.-
Ange they are pazz at that bull-fight to fine
if 'tis his niggah."

"Butt had pawn-*shop!* 'Sieur Davezac,
w'at you 'ave make ad that pawn-*shop?*"

The young man straightened with joy.

But Caroline, outside the double gate, went and came,
describing and explaining

"By those prayer' of my saint, thad monie is raise'! 'Tis now only to fine 'Sieur St.-Ange and give it him. You 'ave the one moiety me I 'ave the other." He backed off.

"Wait, 'Sieur Davezac, wait! My faith! if Posson Jone' don't fine *his* monie, Jules sure to give *those* monie to Posson Jone'!"

Dimitry paused agape while he took in the probability. "Mademoiselle, verie well. I give him that moiety only w'en I see you give him the other."

"But, 'Sieur Davezac, another thing! Père Raphaël, he's come yonder and the judge say 'h-all right.'"

The suitor flamed with wonder and gratitude. "Hah! now to fedge that Jules St.-Ange!" He sped away.

The longest day in the life of Judge St.-

Ange drew to its end. Again the lamplighter
passed. His yellow lights twinkled after
him from corner to corner. Over the darkened shops, and here and there between
them, the balconied windows of one parlor
after another grew luminous inside their
curtains. Only those of the St.-Ange house
remained dark. Tinkling into their melan-
choly dusk with lighted lamps, two servants
in turn had been sent tinkling out of it
again by the solitary judge. "Thad dark-
nezz," he kindly told the second one, "as-
suage' those sore h-eye'."

But now came Caroline. Behind her followed the earlier two; each of the three
bore tall, globed lamps, and at their side
walked his sister.

"My brother," she said, "it is the Sabbath." And as the servants left the lamps

and retired, she added, "Ah, have we not darkness enough, with all those lamp' we can light?"

His inquiry admitted the fact. "Florestine—she is rit-urn'?"

"Florestine she is rit-urn', yes; but better you leave her there w'ere she wild to be al-lone—in her room. St.-Ange, thad Florestine her soul—like mine—is in torment for thad boy, yo' son, my de' brother, oud there in the street."

"He is not in the street, my sister."

The sister clutched her brother's arm in tragic affright, and all at once he lost his self-command, and exclaimed, "My son! —my span'threef!—vagabond!—robber of strenger'!"

"W'ere he is, St.-Ange? Ah, my God! w'at you 'ave done?"

"If that pol-ice 'ave done w'at I sen' them to do, he is in the calaboose."

With a moan as if she were stabbed, the sister sank into a chair and hid her face. The judge rose and pulled a bell-cord, and she hurried out. Before he could speak to the servant who responded, the door-bell rang imperiously.

"Go, you; that 'ave the soun' of M. Davezac. If yes—or if Père Raphaël—tell him come in. Anybody bis-ide, I cann' see them to-night — bic-ause those sore h-eye'. Ah, my God!" he added to himself, "I wizh I 'ave not promize' to play those card'!"

M. Davezac entered with a head as high as if he came with a demand for surrender. What could it mean? At an austere distance he bowed low. Yet the judge made himself almost jovial. "Aha! ad the end you are there for that rip-lye, eh?"

"Rip-lye, m'sieu'?"

"Ah, thad news you wizh me to inform you from Madame Merrifiel'. Sinze several hour' 'tis waiting, thad news. But I like *that*, your dillybration; you will perchanze have the patienze if first I h-ask you some news—of my son."

"M'sieu', 'tis for that I am biffo' you. I h-owe you one debt——"

"'Sieur Davezac, no. My God! if my son was a li'l' mo' like you——"

"If he was a li'l' mo' like me, m'sieu', he would be sleeping to-night in the calaboose, yes."

"My God! young man, you 'ave save' my son from the calaboose?"

PÈRE RAPHAËL

"I 'ave save' who' I can, but yo' good neighbo' of the negs door——"

"Miguel and Joe?"

"They are in the calaboose."

"And Baptiste?"

"In the calaboose."

"And Posson Jone'?"

"In the calaboose."

"And that Collosse of Rhode'?"

"The devil only know'!"

"And Jules?"

"M'sieu', yo' son is ad yo' door."

The father half left his chair, but a painful thought forced him back again. "Young man, young man, you 'ave lent monie to my son—to ruin him worze than biffo'?"

"Lend monie—my faith! I beg him till I sweat!—I beg him till I swear!—I beg him till I cry!—no use! I cannod make him

[138]

to borrow me. All he say, 'My conscien'!
my honor! Pay *my* debt' with *yo'* monie?
Ampossib'!''

Again the judge half left his chair, but
again he restrained himself. "And my son
he is yond' at my door to talk to me ab-out
paying those——"

"No, m'sieu'; he's there to ged that Posson Jone' let out from calaboose."

"Hah!" The judge was disappointed.
"But any'ow, tha' 'z well; I never intan'
Posson Jone' to be put in calaboose. Only
Jules he ought come mo' sooner!"

"No, m'sieu', no uze to come mo' sooner,
till Posson Jone' he 'ave time to sleep off
thad lemonade. And w'iles he's doing that
we try to fine his ole niggah—my soul! we
are nearly *parizh'* with hunting thad black
imbécile."

The judge, his ear quickened by his yearning, suddenly started for the door and as he went its bell softly jingled. But when he opened it, there stood, not his son, but Père Raphaël. If M. Davezac had believed himself caught in a trap set for him he could not have stared with more disconcertion. Suddenly, with scarcely a decent salutation to the newcomer, he said to the judge, "I'll go and fedge yo' son."

But with a kind gesture Père Raphaël detained him, while addressing the judge. "Yo' son? He's not there. But yet he's coming. Only, he rim-ember one other plaze to look for that domestique he's hunting, and he say tell M. Davezac wait till he come."

"Good!" cried the judge, in pure gladness. "And to pazz the time whiles waiting

—card'! Card', Père Raphaël! like this morning arrange'. And the game a three-cornered till Jules come and make it a four!"

Père Raphaël hesitated. "If monsieur," he said, "will pardon me not uncovering the head?—biccause I"—his throat seemed still to be ailing—"I 'ave leave' be'ind me that shed for those sore h-eye."

"Ah, you shall take mine!" cried the host. But that kind of loan was not one for a lender to insist upon, and they sat down to the game as they were. While they were in it to the elbows the door-bell sounded again and Jules St.-Ange presently stood before them. Father and son said a cautiously kind good-evening. The others bowed.

"*Con*-tinue, messieurs," begged the young man, "ah, *con*-tinue the game. I am come only——"

"Ah, we know," said the judge; "but tha' 'z not a nécessaire presently. Come, you shall play, my boy. There is yo' chair, there are yo' counter', waiting sinze the biggening. Come!"

"Ah, no, papa. I like to play you thad game, messieurs, yes; and, beside', I like to win me some monie. To-night tha' 'z the firs' time I ever got use for monie; mais, 'ow I'm goin' to win me anything if all that time I dunno if I'm goin' ged that paper for Posson Jone' to pazz out? Ah, no!"

"For w'at thad Posson Jone' is in calaboose, my son?"

"Papa, he is there for a verie strange; he is lock' for his ril-igion."

"My son! for his ril-igion?"

"'Tis for preaching the specious providence! I know, Père Raphaël, for you that would be a sin, to preach that in the church; but Posson Jone' he di'n' preach that in the church; he preach' it ad thad bull-ring. He thing it is right ad that bull-ring; well, then, ad that bull-ring it is right. Ah, if he 'ave the 'abit to thing that is right, well, he cann' he'p *that;* 'tis his 'abit."

"Assuredlee," murmured Père Raphaël.

"Me, I don't care about those 'abit'," cried the prodigal, with sudden warmth, "if a man stick to his ril-igion and pay his debt'!"

"Ah!" cried the judge, in a glow.

"An' if he can fight like he preach'!" exclaimed M. Davezac.

"Ah, bah!" laughed the judge. "Posson Jone' he fight w'en they try to stop him pritching?"

"Mais certainement," said Jules, "in that

[143]

whole city there is not a priest to fight like that Posson Jone'—exceb'"—he saluted deferentially—"that be Père Raphaël. Bicause, my faith! I bil-ieve he fight juz' as good if he 'ave been sober. And same time *crying*—to pay his debt'!"

"Jules, my boy,"—the judge pointed to an escritoire—"write me there for Posson Jone' to pazz from that calaboose so soon he want'."

"Also Baptiste, papa?" asked Jules, as he labored with the pen.

"Yes, likewise pud that—'also the mulatto boy Baptiste.' Give it me—and the pen."

Presently the pass was in the son's breast-pocket, and the four took up the cards. From the first Père Raphaël had played with a nerve that challenged the judge's admira-

tion, and now at once began to lead the betting with a gentle and taciturn intrepidity.
Dimitry followed with equal daring, the
judge and his son laughed and kept their
caution, and Jules dragged in the constant
and startling losses of the reckless pair. It
seemed but a hop, skip, and jump from the
time they began until these two rose with an
air of resignation.

"Ah!" cried the host, "finish-*ing?* Me,
I am loser al-*so*, but that luck boun' to turn.
We are juz' commance'."

M. Davezac shrugged amusedly and
spread his hands downward. "To commance 'tis enough; I 'ave precisely los' all
I've got there with *me*."

"Me the same," coughed Père Raphaël.

First one and then the other drew forth a
wallet and laid its paper contents uncounted

[145]

before Jules. The prodigal rose, made them into one wad, and with a gracious bow thrust them into the same pocket that held the parson's release. The father rose last, and stood in unconfessed but passionate suspense.

"Well, messieurs," said Jules, saluting as he backed away, "you will egscuse that hurry, with my fran' in that calaboose, and——"

"Jules," responded the judge, following toward the drawing-room door, while Père Raphaël and Davezac drew away in opposite directions, "you don't need to go if you——" He felt a touch on his arm; his sister stood beside him.

"Jules," she interposed, "if you 'ave there already not quite enough to pud you out of debt——"

"Tante,—papa,"—the son drew forth his gains—"I win that in yo' 'ouse, and from fran'. You thing that be honorab' to pay that to shopkipper? My faith, that is a secred!" He looked round to appeal the point to Père Raphaël, but the hooded figure had vanished, and Davezac stood between him and his kindred, heaving with indignation. "M'sieu' St.-Ange!" said Dimitry.

Jules smiled fondly. "M'sieu' Davezac?"

"You know w'at I would say, me, if that was not yo' 'ouse here?"

"'Tis not my 'ouse. W'at that is you would say?"

"I would say, take that monie and pay those debt', or fight me under those live-oak', Bayou St. Jean, to-morrow sun-*rise!*"

The prodigal smiled on. "I meet you

there. My faith! tha' 'z the first time I ever got use for monie, and then you thing I'm goin' teck it and pay my *debt*? Ah, m'sieu', I be sorry to fighd you for that, but—'tis a matt' of conscien'!"

The speaker's last glimpse of the company as he left them showed the judge turning fiercely upon Davezac, and his aunt heatedly arraigning her brother. Surely he would not have shut himself out had he seen his father, at the instant of the door's closing, saved from a fall only by the arms of Tante and Florestine as the latter darted into the room, or had he heard himself imperatively called by the weeping girl.

The judge recovered himself, lifted the shade from his eyes, painfully blinked around the room, and spoke with dignity. "M'sieu' Davezac—Père Raphaël——"

But not even Tante or Florestine remained to reply. Only Caroline responded: "Miché Dabzac an' Père Raphaël done gone, miché. Yass, suh, by de po'te-cochère." A statement, like history, only partly true.

Once more the market-houses sparkled with candles, resounded with cheerful discords. Out on Bayou Road, in the sky that overarched suburb St. Jean, the Sabbath night faded into day. Under one of the bayou's vast oaks stood Caroline, casting frightened eyes everywhere and speaking warily to some one out of sight. "Dis bound to be de place," she said; "yondeh de schooneh; but no pahson, an' no Miché Jules. Lawd, sen' 'em quick! Look' to me like ow dough done cook' when I see de jedge an' po' ole momselle leave de house

afo' day, but when dey tu'n' off to look up
Father Pierre I praise' G— Good Lawd,
yondeh come Miché Dabzac!"

"Hi-ide!" stealthily called her hidden con-
federate, but Dimitry had seen her.

"Mawnin', Miché Dabzac," the maid
pertly saluted, "mawnin', suh."

With a stately frown he signed to her to
speak more quietly, and she obeyed, though
with a show of amusement.

"D' ain't nobody here 'cep' you an' me,
an' us all done ruin' now, anyhow, 'less 'n
I can waylay Pahson Jone' an' 'suade
him fo' to not let Miché Jules give him
dat ah monie. Dass all Miss Flo'stine
'ould eveh sen' me out here faw at dis
scan'lous hour."

"Then go you back. Tell her he shall not
give it, I shall privvent him!"

"Lawd, miché, but s'posin' he done gi'n it to him already."

"He shall give it him back. Go you at home; tha' 'z nod the place for you here. My faith! militraise, I bil-ieve you are there only to fine that vilain Baptiste."

"I swear I ain't! I ain't see' dat fool sence de middle o' de night, when he set off ag'in to try to scare up Pahson Jone' ole niggeh."

"Go you at home, Caroline."

"Miché Dabzac, I see' Miss Abby sence I see' you las'."

The maid backed enticingly toward the trunk of the oak; the young man followed.

"Yass, suh; las' evenin', when y' all gone, Père Raphaël an' all, Miss Flo'stine writ me a pass an' slipp' me out fo' to run tell Miss Abby an' her ma how Miché Jules 'fuse to pay his debt', an' w'at pass mo'oveh 'twix' him an' you——"

"Ah, ah! she 'ave no ri-ight!"

"Hol' on! hol' on! De Lawd move' her to do it. I fine 'em confessin' dey conscience to one 'notheh, Madame Mayfiel' a-sobbin' 'caze she been to Catholic church, and Miss Abby 'caze o' de way we raise dat ah monie; an' when I tell 'em o' dis yeh las' pickle you done got us in——"

"Me? me? me?"

"Oh, yass, suh; yass, suh; yass, suh! When you tell Miché Jules he got to pay or fight, ain't he dess djuty-bound to fight and to not pay, fo' to p'otec' his honoh? You dess ax Miss Flo'stine!"

"Ah, bah! He can pay firz' and fight after."

The maid started with surprise, but then

laughed. "My sakes! miché, he wouldn'
think o' dat in fi-ive years. And when I told
dem po' ladies what you done, dey dess drap'
'pon one 'notheh an' cry like dey heart—
Lawd! yondeh Madame Mayfiel' now!"

"Diable! go you at home!"

"Too late; she done spied me. Oh, now
we is gone done it to de las' lick! Here she
come to stop de djuel, an' fine nobody 'cep'
we two togetheh! Fo' Gawd's sake! ef you
got yo' djuelin'-tools hid away anywhuz
round here, run fetch 'em out an' parade
'em all you kin!

"Mawnin', Madame Mayfiel'. Lawd!
you out here alone?"

"Oh, Caroline, where is my daughter?
Where is Abigail? And why does Mr.
Davezac avoid me?"

"Lawd! Madame Mayfiel', he think 'tis

Miché Jules comin', an' he dess gone git his djuelin'-tools."

The young man reappeared. He bowed superbly to Mrs. Merrifield, but glared on Caroline. "Misérable! Who has stole me those sword' from the hole of thad tree?"

"Swords!" gasped the frightened lady, at which the youth bowed again and then stiffened high.

"Madame, if that is by yo' command——"

Her brows lifted with distress. "No, sir, no, no! I've overstepped, but I haven't stolen—oh, who can tell me where is my daughter?"

"Lawd A'mighty!" cried Caroline, "ain't she home in bed?"

"Bed? We've neither of us touched one! At daylight I left her and went to market——"

PÈRE RAPHAËL

The alarmed Davezac pressed close. "You leff her?"

"She begged me to go! It was to find you! Oh, sir, I'll buy off the pawnbroker if only you'll not fight until we've got everything back into the judge's house!"

"But yo' daughteh! yo' daughteh! when you have ritturn'?"

"I found her note. She'd seen Father Pierre passing, called him in and told him all! And she's gone with him, writing me that I'd understand! But I don't, and I can't, and I'm afraid something dreadful has——"

"Ah, madame, with Father Pierre, no! They 'ave gone perchanze ad the judge. I'll go there and——"

He sprang to go, but at the second stride halted squarely before the small, cowled figure of Père Raphaël, who had issued from a clump of bushes holding out to him the missing swords. "You are forgettingg?"

"Yes! I was forgettingg!"

"Or maybee you don't want to fighd some mo', and finding egscuze to leave?"

The young man snatched the swords and swelled for a fitting retort from a Creole gentleman to a priest of his faith; but before he could find it Mrs. Merrifield and Caroline rushed in between them, panting in fright and shame, "The judge! the judge and his sister!"

The judge and his sister arrived at high speed, she with her hair in her eyes, he with his green shade on one ear. "Florestine!" they called. "Florestine, she's not here? Where is Florestine? Ah, Madame Merrifiel', Florestine is gone with Jules! Jules have rob' the 'ouse and gone with Florestine!"

But the distracted mother scarcely heard them, for yet another pair came after them in close pursuit, and with a moan of joy she sprang from the group into the arms of Abigail beside Father Pierre, while Caroline tearfully cried to the judge and his sister, "Momselle Flo'stine all right, mawsteh! She safe, mist'ess! She *all right!* I swah to Gawd she all right! You kin ax Père Rapha'—o-o-oh, Lawd, but dis *is* de Lawd's own doin's! Yondeh Miché Jules and de piney-wood' pahson!"

Amid these preoccupations Father Pierre, hurriedly drawn aside by Père Raphaël, received from that small informant swift assertions that visibly amazed him, and propositions to which he nevertheless eagerly consented. As Jules, the parson, and Baptiste came into view engrossed in the wel-

come sight of the *Isabella* schooner, Father
Pierre waved back the couples about him.
"We are too mannie, ladies and gen'le-
men. Back, iv you please—and even you,
judge. Père Raphaël and me we are sue-
ficient."

Père Raphaël was already moving toward
Jules and the parson, and Father Pierre followed. At the vessel's side Parson Jones
paused to pledge Jules a lifelong affection.
Grouped with the ladies and Davezac the
judge was holding himself well in hand; but
when he witnessed the love and admiration
his boy had won from a stranger and the
remotest of aliens, his *sine quâ non* crumbled
at last, and to the bounding joy of all behind
him, "Father Pierre!" he warily called, "a
word, a word, not more! Say to Père Raphaël he can tell my son if he *say* he goin'

[158]

pay those debt' with those monie everything
be all right. To commance, 'tis enough!"

With a gay nod Father Pierre motioned
him off and pressed nearer Père Raphaël.
Before they could come close, Jules, following the schooner as with limp sails she moved
along the shore to the poling of her crew—
but all that is of earlier record: how his
card-table winnings were offered the parson
and declined; how Colossus reappeared and
what he did; how Jules swore, laughed,
and wept, and how, as the schooner finally
bore away his God-sent friend, he stood and
gazed after its fading topmasts.

While he so stood, his father, oblivious of
all bystanders, the green shade lost and
"those sore h-eye'" forgotten, stood and
gazed on him with a sympathy as keen and
evident as his yearning suspense; and if the

observance of these emotions intensified the sympathy and suspense of every one, what words shall tell their raptures when they saw Jules at length turn and say, "Baptiste, you know what I goin' do wid dis monie?"

"Non, miché."

"Well, you can strike me dead if I don't goin' to pay all my debts."

He began a little song, if you remember; but while its opening measure was still on his tongue, at the first townward bend of the path, the whole glad flock of his seekers, with the judge at their front, stopped his way.

"Papa!" exclaimed the joyous prodigal

"My son!" cried the father. "An egs-change! a fair egschange! Yo' absolution for mine!"

So they came into each other's arms. Yet

in the next breath they were half apart again.
"But Florestine?" they cried in one breath,
"ah, where—" Both voices were silenced
by Jules's amazement at something hap-
pening behind his father, and the judge, turning, stared, with his son, upon Père Raphaël
frantically clasping and kissing—*kissing*, do
you realize it?—kissing and embracing
Tante, Abigail, Mrs. Merrifield and even
Caroline. But cowl and eye-shade had been
crowded off the face and head, and these
were the face and head of Florestine.

"Forgive you, my child?" the aunt was
exclaiming. "Ah, betteh you h-ask somebody betteh than me; for, me, I only fine
that out, that robb'rie, when, too late, I
commance' to make the same thing myseff."

"To commance," sighed the happy girl to
Father Pierre as they all turned homeward

together, "'tis enough. Me, the same like Jules, I am discourage' to be wicked any mo', those Providence get al-ong so well without."